Ruth watched her for a moment, and then came over. Bending down next to Lola, she said in a low voice, 'I know it's none of my business, but if there is something going on, then I'm glad.'

﹖ glanced at her, surprised.

⸺ smiled. 'Harry's got so many barriers up, it'd be good to see someone break through them. He's such a nice boy underneath it all, but he hasn't had many pe⸻ ⸺ about him.'

⸺ Lola looked at the ground again, feeling ⸺thing flutter in her stomach.

'ou seem like a really nice girl too,' said Ruth, still keeping her voice low. 'Maybe you'd be good for Harry.'

Read all the

stories!

**Star Crossed**
**Strictly Friends?**
**Forget Me Not**
**Ice Dreams**
**Model Behaviour**

Coming soon:
**Deep Water**

SWEET HEARTS: MODEL BEHAVIOUR
A RED FOX BOOK 978 1 849 41218 6

First published in Great Britain by Red Fox Books,
an imprint of Random House Children's Books,
A Random House Group Company

This edition published 2012

1 3 5 7 9 10 8 6 4 2

Copyright © Jo Cotterill, 2012
Cover artwork copyright © Helen Huang 2012

The right of Jo Cotterill to be identified as the author of this work has been
asserted in accordance with the Copyright, Designs and Patents Act 1988.

The Random House Group Limited supports The Forest Stewardship Council
(FSC®), the leading international forest certification organization. Our books
carrying the FSC label are printed on FSC®-certified paper. FSC is the only forest
certification scheme endorsed by the leading environmental organizations,
including Greenpeace. Our paper procurement policy can be found
at www.randomhouse.co.uk/environment

Set in Birka 12/15.5pt by Falcon Art Graphic

Red Fox Books are published by Random House Children's Books,
61–63 Uxbridge Road, London W5 5SA

www.kidsatrandomhouse.co.uk
www.totallyrandombooks.co.uk

Addresses for companies within The Random House Group Limited
can be found at: www.randomhouse.co.uk/offices.htm

THE RANDOM HOUSE GROUP Limited Reg. No. 954009

A CIP catalogue record for this book is available from the British Library.

Printed and bound by CPI Group (UK) Ltd, Croydon, CR0 4YY

*For everyone at the Oxfordshire
Animal Sanctuary, with thanks*

# Chapter 1

## such an opportunity!

'I can't *wait*,' exclaimed Lola, stepping into the crystal-clear water and letting herself sink gradually into its warmth. 'Do you think they'd let me design something? I've got this idea for a new bag, you see . . .'

'You don't know which department you'll be working in, though,' her best friend Naiha pointed out. 'You might be put in something really boring, like Pattern Cutting.'

Lola floated on her back and looked up at her friend. They were both tall and slim and beautiful, but Lola was all English Rose with her pale skin and long blonde hair, whereas Naiha's Indian heritage gave her skin the colour of chocolate milkshake and hair as glossy and black as treacle. 'I wouldn't mind. Pattern cutting is really important. But I hope Marisa lets me work in Design.'

'It's lucky your mum is friends with her. I mean,

work experience at Mulberry is, like, really hard to get.' Naiha kicked off her flip-flops and dropped her towel onto a bench. She was wearing a bright yellow bikini, in contrast to Lola's red gingham swimming costume. 'I hope the water is warmer today.'

'It is.' Lola grinned. 'I shivered so much after our last swim, Corin thought I'd caught a chill. He came and turned up the thermostat straight away.' The two girls laughed.

'Your stepdad is a big softy,' said Naiha, stepping carefully into the water. 'He'd buy you the moon if you wanted it.'

'I know. But it's not just me. He's soft with everyone. Mum says it's a wonder that his health clubs haven't all gone bankrupt because he's not tough enough for business.' Lola smiled. 'He's sweet. I can hardly remember what it was like before he came along, to be honest. Louder, I think – and Mum was a bit wilder. But he's a great stepdad, even if he does bang on about having five fruit and vegetables every day. And exercise, of course.'

'You are so lucky to have a pool in your house,' Naiha said enviously. 'I've been trying to tell Mum we need one too, but she just rolls her eyes and comes out with one of her Indian proverbs. "The money you dream about won't pay the bills", or something like that.'

'I thought your dad sent money from India?'

'He does. He's rolling in it! But Mum's always tutting and saying he doesn't give her enough. Do you know how much his last film made? *Millions!*'

Lola swam lazily around in a circle. 'Bet you can't wait to see him next week.'

'I totally can't. It's actually *happening*, Lola. For, like, the first time ever, I'm actually going to see him at work! *And* he says he'll introduce me to Mallika Shan!'

'Who?'

'You know, that amazing Bollywood actress? The one I said was like the Cameron Diaz of the Indian film world?'

'Oh, right. Yeah, I remember.' Lola wasn't entirely sure she did, but she didn't want to upset her friend. Naiha talked about her father's films a lot, and sometimes Lola found it hard to stay interested. 'When did you last see your dad?'

Naiha pulled a face. 'Not for ages. I was supposed to be going out there last summer, but . . .'

'I know.' Lola felt sorry for her. Naiha's dad wasn't the most reliable of people and her friend had been let down badly last year. 'But it's all sorted this time, isn't it? You're really going!'

Naiha grinned. 'Miss Bourne's face when I said I was going to do my work experience in Bollywood! She nearly fell off her chair!'

'I don't think she's used to glamorous stuff,' replied Lola.

'You can tell that by her hairstyle,' said Naiha, rolling her eyes.

'Naiha! Don't be mean!'

'It is awful, though – come on. That thick fringe.' Naiha shuddered.

Lola couldn't help smiling. 'It is a bit dire. I bet Shallika whatshername wouldn't be seen dead with her hair like that.'

'*Mallika Shan.* Honestly, Lola, you're so dippy, you never remember anything.'

'I remember things that are *important*,' said Lola in a teasing voice. Then she giggled, and Naiha did too. 'So, do you think you'll get to be in a scene in your dad's film?'

'That's what I'm hoping,' agreed Naiha. 'I thought I'd just hang around the edges and then, when they're saying, *Oh no, we need another person here, but there isn't anyone* . . . I'd step in and say, "I'm here! I can do it!"'

'That would be the most amazing thing ever.' Lola's eyes shone. 'I'd love to be in a film.'

'Me too.' Naiha sighed.

Both girls silently contemplated their reflections in the shiny ceiling. The pool room was large, with a pair of white pillars at one end. Several reclining pool chairs took up the space along one wall, and two changing rooms and a sauna occupied the other end. Naiha sighed again.

'If I could get on a model agency's books, it would be a great way into films. Can't you talk to your people again?'

Lola pulled a face. 'I did try, Naiha. It's not my fault they said no.'

'I know.'

'Besides,' added Lola kindly, 'it's not as if I do much modelling work myself yet.'

'Not as much as meee!' came a voice from the steps leading up to the kitchen, and Sienna Cassidy, Lola's younger sister, came bouncing down. 'Did I tell you I'm going to do another H&M shoot?'

Lola felt hurt. 'Why didn't they ask me?' The two girls had signed with the same agency three years ago. It had seemed a natural thing to do, following in their mother's footsteps, and it was good fun, trying on the clothes and posing for the camera. But recently, Sienna had been called for more jobs than Lola, and it was beginning to rankle.

'You're too old.' Sienna stuck out her tongue. 'They were looking for twelve-year-olds.'

'Oh.'

'H&M is all right,' said Naiha. 'They've got some good stuff.'

'Yeah, it's cool!' Sienna beamed. Like Lola, she had straight blonde hair and long legs. 'And last time they let me keep some of the clothes.' She jerked a thumb towards the stairs. 'Corin's out this evening and Mum says she can't be bothered to cook, so we're having Thai takeaway.'

Lola cheered up. 'Brilliant. Can we have some of that raita bread?'

'I expect so. Mum's just bunged in the same order as we had last time, I think. She's still working on the launch. Says the caterers are charging far too much and she's mad at Cleo for hiring them.'

Lola and Sienna's mother, Helena Cassidy, had been a successful model in the 80s and since then had dabbled in almost every area in the fashion world, from shoes to bags, make-up to accessories. Her latest project was 'Helena's Whisper', a new perfume to add to her range which already included 'Helena's Blush' and 'Helena's Kiss'. The perfume was due to be launched in six weeks at a swanky hotel, and Helena was spending hours every day on the phone or computer in her study, alternately cajoling and threatening her personal assistant.

'I'm coming in,' Sienna announced, before disappearing into a cubicle and emerging seconds later clad in a sky-blue tankini with silver sequins on the straps.

'That's mine!' exclaimed Lola.

'Not any more,' Sienna told her. 'It fits me perfectly.'

Lola frowned at her sister. 'You should have asked.'

'What for? *You* didn't ask when you borrowed my straighteners yesterday.'

'What have you got planned for next week?' asked Naiha hastily, anxious to ward off a sisterly argument.

'Shopping, mostly.' Sienna shrugged. 'Meeting up with my friends. Watching loads of TV and going to Pret.'

'Boring,' commented Lola, though secretly she was jealous of her sister's plans for half term. It sounded like the sort of thing she'd have liked to do herself, if she hadn't been going to work at such a prestigious design house. She felt her stomach flutter with excitement again. *Mulberry!* It was such an opportunity! She adored textiles, photography and art at school – surely the perfect combination for a future career in fashion? And she'd finally get to see behind the scenes; perhaps be able to decide whether design was more important to her than modelling . . . it was so hard to choose!

'It sounds cool,' said Naiha. 'You know I'm going out to India to work with my dad, don't you? For work experience.'

'Yeah, I know, you've only told me about fifty times.' Sienna grinned. 'Have you started packing?'

'I *have*, actually,' Naiha told her. 'But I've already filled two suitcases and I haven't even packed shoes yet!'

'Bollywood,' said Sienna, shaking her head in wonder. '*So* cool. Much cooler than Hollywood.'

'Totally.' Naiha nodded. 'Hollywood is so *yesterday*. Isn't it, Lola?'

'Hm?' Lola blinked. She had been in the middle of imagining her first day at Mulberry. 'What?'

Naiha laughed. 'Earth to Lola, come in, Lola!'

'Sorry, I was miles away.' Lola looked embarrassed. 'What did you say?'

'I said Bollywood is cooler than Hollywood, right?'

'Oh – oh, yeah.' Lola knew Naiha wanted her to agree, so she did. But she wasn't *entirely* sure why Bollywood was better . . .

'So you'll be out there, mixing with the stars,' said Sienna with a sigh, 'while Lola jams herself onto the Tube in London and tries not to breathe in.'

'The Tube isn't that bad,' said Lola defensively. 'And anyway, it's only three stops from Quinn's place.'

The eldest of the Cassidy girls, Quinn was twenty and lived in her own flat in London. Lola and Sienna envied her more than anything because Quinn was a successful model, sometimes doing shoots in exotic locations like Iceland or Antigua. She had agreed to put Lola up for the week while she was on work experience, and Lola couldn't wait to stay with her sister.

'I wish I was staying with Quinn,' Sienna said.

Lola felt warm inside. 'She said she'd take me to this really amazing design gallery, where they show stuff by new designers – you know, graduates. Sometimes you can buy their creations too.' The excited feeling in her stomach grew, like a bubble. She hadn't told anyone, but Lola was planning to pack a couple of her own designs too – a bag and a belt – that she'd created all by herself. How amazing would it be if one of the London people liked her work! 'You're an undiscovered talent . . .' they would say. 'As soon as you finish school, you must come and work for us . . .'

'*Lola.*'

'Hm – what?'

Naiha was shaking her head. 'You're doing it again. Didn't you hear me?'

'Sorry.' Lola pulled a face. 'I don't know what's got into me today. I'm too excited about next week, that's all.'

Naiha rolled her eyes. 'Sienna was saying Quinn went to a Lady Gaga party the other weekend. For her latest single.'

'Did she?' Lola felt hurt. Quinn hadn't told her that – or had she? Had Lola been daydreaming again and missed it?

'She got papped,' said Sienna importantly. 'You know, photographed by the paparazzi.'

'I *do* know what it means . . .'

'And she said it ended up in a London magazine! Her, standing next to Marvin from JLS and she hadn't even realized!' Sienna did a half-hearted attempt at front crawl for a few strokes, and then turned to announce, 'I might be a fashion journalist when I grow up.'

'I thought you were going to be a model,' said Naiha.

'Yes, I am. Well, probably. But I'd like to write for magazines too. You know they get free stuff sent to them all the time? Just for writing reviews of things.'

'You hate writing!' Lola pointed out.

'I hate writing at *school*,' argued her sister. 'That's not proper writing, though, is it? I mean, I can't do a review of Maybelline's latest mascara for school, can I?'

Lola grinned. 'Don't think the teacher would like it.'

'No. Especially if it was meant to be about Romeo and Juliet.' Sienna giggled. 'I had to read the balcony scene yesterday with Rufus. It was sooo embarrassing.'

'Hello!' came a voice from the stairs.

'Hello, Samir!' the three girls called back. 'We're down here,' added Lola. It was a nice surprise to see her boyfriend – Samir was always cheerful and he never failed to tell her she looked good.

Samir came down the steps, grinning. 'I guessed,' he said. His tanned skin and golden curly hair seemed to glow in the reflection of the pool. Walking down to the girls, he looked like a Greek god, even in jeans and a T-shirt. 'Can I come in?'

'Mum's ordered Thai,' Lola said. 'I don't know when it's coming.'

'OK,' Samir said, pulling off his top. 'Then I'll have to be quick.' He disappeared into a cubicle and within seconds reappeared in green swimming shorts. 'Which part of the pool shall I bomb today?' His mouth twisted into a mischievous grin.

The girls shrieked. 'Don't you dare!' Lola shouted. 'I've got make-up on!'

'I don't want my hair wet—' Sienna started to say, but Samir had already taken a leap from the side. Tucked into a ball, he smashed into the water, sending droplets everywhere.

'You pig!' screamed Sienna as Samir resurfaced, laughing. 'I can't believe you did that!' But there was a lack of conviction to her voice. Everyone liked Samir. He was always welcome at the Cassidy house. Even Corin, who was noticeably protective of his stepdaughters, approved of Lola's boyfriend.

Samir swam over to Lola and reached out. *The sweetie*, thought Lola, *he wants to kiss me!* She offered her cheek, but only received a hearty splash instead. 'Gaaah!'

Samir laughed again. 'Gotcha!'

'You are such a pain, Samir.' Sienna was giggling. *She fancies him too*, Lola thought to herself. *Almost all the girls I know fancy him. But he's going out with me!* The thought that she and Samir were the 'golden couple' of their year made her happy. They'd only been going out for a few months, but Lola's friends were already planning the wedding, and sometimes

Lola found herself practising her married signature: *Lola Hopestone* had a nice ring to it . . .

Sienna stood up at the shallow end and flicked her hair over her shoulder, gathering the long blonde locks in her hands and squeezing out the water. 'Samir,' she said, just to make sure he was watching, 'what are you doing for work experience?'

Lola and Naiha exchanged amused glances. 'He's working at Next,' said Lola, her voice sympathetic. 'Poor thing.'

'It'll be cool,' said Samir, missing the undertone. 'I'll be in the menswear department.'

'He's going to be a *shop assistant*,' Naiha elaborated for Sienna.

Sienna gave Samir her most beaming smile. 'It sounds great. Next stuff is classic.'

Samir beamed back. 'Yeah, it's cool.' *At least I don't have to worry about him fancying other girls*, thought Lola to herself. *He never seems to notice that they like him!* 'And it's better than what my dad offered me. I'd rather work in a shop than sit in a boring courtroom all day.'

'Isn't someone at school doing that?' Naiha asked Lola.

Lola nodded. 'Fenella. She wants to be a lawyer, though.'

'Square.'

Lola shrugged. 'She likes that kind of thing.'

'I think being in court could be kind of cool,' Sienna interrupted, still smiling at Samir. 'You know, all those murders.'

'There are hardly any murders really,' Samir told her. 'So Dad says. It's all boring stuff about not paying tax and stealing cars.'

Sienna looked disappointed. 'But you're always hearing about murders on the news.'

'Have you seen the new *Glamour* yet?' asked Naiha, looking bored and changing the subject. 'There's a whole feature on dry skin in winter.'

'Exactly what we were talking about last week!' Lola said, wiping water from her eyes.

'I know! We have to exfoliate more, that's what it says.'

'Boring!' called Samir. As Lola turned to look at him, he gave her a cheeky grin. 'Who's first for a ducking?'

'No, no, no!' cried Lola as Samir dived under the water and headed towards her. 'My mascara's not waterproof!'

But it was too late – Samir had already reached her legs and given a big tug. Lola slipped and sank under the water, her blonde hair floating out around her head like a halo. She surfaced, gasping. 'You idiot! I'm going to look like a panda now!'

Samir surfaced beside her. 'You always look beautiful to me.'

'Oh, shut up.'

'You're next, Naiha!'

Naiha screamed. 'Don't you dare!' She turned and thrashed her way towards the steps.

Samir laughed. 'Gotcha!' He turned to Lola. 'I got picked for the rugby team, by the way.'

'Huh.' Lola was still squeezing the water from her streaming hair. Inside, she was pleased to hear the news, but she wanted Samir to think she was still cross over ducking her. She couldn't be seen to forgive him *that* easily, could she?

'Wow!' Sienna went into impress-Samir mode again. 'That's amazing! You must be so good! And rugby is so much cooler than football anyway.'

'No, it isn't,' countered Naiha, climbing out of the pool. 'You never hear about rugby players' wives, do you?'

Both she and Sienna turned to look at Lola meaningfully. 'What?' asked Lola.

Samir grinned at her. 'Would you rather marry a rugby player or a footballer?'

Lola flushed. 'I don't want to marry anyone right

now, thank you!' Inside, she felt a bit excited. Was Samir thinking of marriage in the future too? They were too young now, of course, but his question was suggestive. Wait till Tasha and Alisha heard! Lola went off into another daydream, this time imagining herself being interviewed for *Hello* magazine. 'Well, of course,' she would say sweetly, 'I never had the tiniest idea he was going to propose! But there was this one time, years ago, when we were in the swimming pool, and he kind of hinted that one day he might . . . But it was still the biggest shock when he got down on one knee at the top of the Eiffel Tower!'

'Curry's here!' her mother's voice echoed from upstairs. Lola blinked, brought back to reality with a snap.

'Oh, pants,' Sienna said. 'I haven't got time to dry my hair.'

Samir shrugged. 'What for?'

'Oh, do you think it looks all right?' Sienna twisted a strand around her finger.

'Yeah.'

She beamed.

Naiha rolled her eyes at Lola. 'We have *got* to get you a boyfriend,' she said to Sienna.

Sienna blushed. 'I wouldn't go out with just anyone. I'd need to be totally into him.'

'I know what you mean,' Samir agreed, looking at Lola. Sienna's face fell and Lola turned away, feeling her mouth curve into a smile. How could she possibly stay mad at Samir when he was just so incredibly sweet?

There was a slight tinkling noise, and the four of them turned to see Helena Cassidy making her way gently down the stairs. She still had that model's way of 'making an entrance'. Her posture was perfect and she crossed her legs as she walked, as though she were permanently on a catwalk. Her make-up was so skillfully done you'd have sworn she wasn't wearing any at all, but Lola and Sienna knew how long it took to perfect that look. Their mother was wearing a long silk kimono and her new perfume, which smelled of jasmine and white musk. 'Hello, darlings. Did you hear me call about the curry?'

'Yes,' said Sienna. 'I was going to dry my hair.'

'You won't have time, sweetie. Borrow my hair towel. You'll just have to look like you've come from the spa.' Helena smiled, revealing perfect pearly-white teeth. Then she turned to Lola. 'Darling, I need to talk to you about something.'

Naiha and Samir disappeared into the cubicles. Lola reached for a large purple towel and started rubbing her hair. 'What is it?'

'Your work experience.' Helena's voice sounded puzzled, though her face retained its smooth perfection. 'I've just got off the phone to Marisa. She mentioned the photoshoot they're doing next week – you know, the summer stuff – and I said, "Do you think Lola would be allowed to go along?" And she said, "What do you mean?" And I said, "When she's on work experience, of course." And she said, "I don't know what you're talking about, we never had her application form."' Helena's eyes grew large and luminous. 'You *did* send it in, didn't you?'

Lola wrapped the towel tightly around her body. 'Of course I did. I mean—' A horrible memory suddenly broke in. A three-page form, with boxes to fill in and explanations to give and *Why I Want To Work At Mulberry*. Sitting on her desk in her room . . . pushed aside to make room for *Vogue* magazine . . . 'Oh God.' A chill swept over her.

'Oh, Lola.' Helena's tone was disapproving. 'Why on earth didn't you sort it out?'

Lola felt slightly sick. 'I thought, since Marisa said she'd fix it for me . . .' Dread made her angry. 'Why would I need to fill in a stupid form? *You* said it was all sorted.'

'No,' Helena replied firmly. 'I said I'd asked Marisa and she'd said it would be fine. But she did add that you needed to fill in a form, just like all the other applicants. To make it official. I assumed, since you didn't say anything, that you'd done it.'

'Surely she can fit me in? I mean, can't you just ask . . . ?'

'No, I can't,' Helena said. 'She's got two work experience girls for next week already. They can't take any more.'

A horrible silence settled over the room, only broken by the slight lapping of the pool water against the tiled sides.

*I can't believe it.* Lola's mind raced around in circles. *I've lost my placement at Mulberry. All my dreams of working with the top designers – ruined! This is the biggest disaster of my life!*

# Chapter 2

## getting your hands dirty will be good for you

'I won't go,' Lola said stubbornly. 'It's ridiculous.'

Her form teacher, Miss Bourne, was exasperated. 'It's your own fault, Lola. You assured us you had fixed it up yourself. You've only yourself to blame.'

Lola muttered about stupid paperwork and stupid people.

'You can't expect us to be able to place you at a top fashion house with only two days' notice,' Miss Bourne told her. 'The Parchester Animal Sanctuary is a wonderful place, and they have a great record of work experience. We send people there every year – it's only this year that no one expressed an interest in working with animals.'

'I don't know anything about animals,' complained Lola. 'And I get scared when dogs bark.'

'Then maybe it's time you toughened up a bit,' Miss Bourne said unsympathetically. 'Honestly, Lola, you live in cloud-cuckoo-land half the time. Getting your hands dirty will be good for you. Now, off you go.'

'Can't I just stay home instead?'

'No, you can't,' Miss Bourne snapped. 'This is a requirement of the school, and it will provide material for your English assignments, as you very well know. You're just going to have to knuckle down and get on with it. It's only for a week.'

Lola stomped out of the classroom, her face red with anger. Naiha was waiting outside.

'What did she say?'

Lola felt close to tears. 'She says I've got to work at some animal sanctuary next week. That it's all the school could find me at the last minute.'

'An animal sanctuary?' Naiha looked bewildered. 'But that's . . . I mean . . . couldn't they find you some kind of art or design place? They know you're good at textiles and stuff like that.'

Lola shrugged and kicked at the floor. 'She said it was too short notice. She was really mean, actually.'

'You poor thing.' Naiha patted her on the arm. 'I'm so sorry.'

'It's all right for you,' Lola said vehemently. '*You're* off to Bollywood.'

'Yeah . . .'

'And Tasha's working at the BBC, and Alisha's a runner at a music studio. I'm going to be the only one with a rubbish work experience.' Her eyes filled with tears again. 'It is *so* unfair.'

♥

'I didn't know Parchester even had an animal sanctuary,' commented Corin, at dinner.

His wife turned to him. 'Of course you did, darling. I did a photoshoot there once, don't you remember? For the charity calendar? I had to sit with some cats and this vile feline dug its claws into my legs and ripped my tights.'

Corin looked blank. 'Nope, don't remember. Pass the rice, Sienna.'

'This is nice,' Helena said, biting the head off a king prawn. 'What is it?'

'Nigel Slater chilli and lime recipe,' Corin replied. 'Good, isn't it?'

'I've told Miss Bourne I won't go,' Lola said, determined to keep the conversation focused on her problem.

Helena looked surprised. 'Why?'

'Because I don't want to, all right?' Lola felt her voice tremble. 'I really, really want to work at Mulberry.'

To her horror, her eyes filled with tears. 'I want to work at a design house . . .' *Like in my dream . . .*

'Lola, sweetie, we know you're upset,' said Corin. 'But what's done is done. If I'd known earlier, I could have fixed up something for you at the club, but there's no chance now. The school has done its best to find you something at short notice. You'll just have to put up with it, I'm afraid.'

Lola bit her lip and stared at the table, willing the tears not to fall.

'Maybe there's another way,' said her mother. 'Why don't we ask Marisa when the next gap is coming up and you can go to Mulberry then?'

Hope rushed through Lola. 'Could we? I could take a week off school then, it wouldn't matter. And then I wouldn't have to go next week.'

Corin shook his head. 'You can't just take a week off whenever you feel like it, Lola. Your schoolwork is important. You can reapply to Mulberry, I'm sure. Maybe go in the holidays instead.'

Helena sighed. 'Corin's right, darling. You'll just have to make the best of it. I'm sure it won't be as bad as you think.'

Lola's heart, which had leaped at a possible way out, sank again.

'I think working with animals is cool,' Sienna

commented, helping herself to more salad. 'All those cute cats and rabbits and things. You'll probably just have to sit there and stroke them. I mean, what can there actually be to do all day? It's not like it can be that hard to feed them and let them hop around, can it?'

Lola thought about it. 'I guess you could be right.' Visions of puppies and kittens swam before her eyes. Maybe she could take her camera and practise photographing them. Or get someone to photograph her with the animals, like the photoshoot her mum had done. She knew just how she'd set up the shot – one fluffy cat draped lazily over her shoulder, while she gazed out at the camera . . .

'I think you'll probably find it harder work than you're expecting,' her stepdad was saying. 'But I think it's an excellent idea. Where is this place, anyway?'

'It's on South Park Road,' Lola said.

Corin brightened. 'Well, that's handy. I can drop you there on my way to work in the morning and pick you up afterwards.'

'Have you told Quinn?' asked Helena suddenly. 'That you're not coming up, I mean?'

'Oh – no, no, I haven't.' Lola didn't explain why she hadn't rung her sister. She had been hoping, right up until the last minute, that something could have been sorted out. But maybe it would be all right, after all. And she could still go to Mulberry in the future, couldn't she? Maybe if she went in the holidays she could go for longer than a week? Maybe they'd even offer her a temporary post . . .

The phone rang from a distant room. Helena half rose, but Corin reached out to touch her arm. 'Can't it wait?'

She hesitated. 'I suppose so.' She sat down. 'It's bound to be Cleo again.'

'How are the plans for the launch?'

Helena grimaced. 'Foul. Cleo is being absolutely useless. I told her to tell the decorators that we wanted pink fairy lights – next thing I know we've got silver chandeliers! And the caterers just keep pushing up the prices because of the dietary requirements. I mean, honestly, is it too much to expect professional caterers to provide gluten- and dairy-free options?' She shook her head. 'And some woman called Vivienne has been ringing me up and offering her services. She's setting up as an events organizer – as if I'd use someone who's never done it before! I tell you, the whole thing is enough to give me a migraine.'

'Are we coming?' asked Sienna.

Helena looked surprised. 'Of course you are,

darling. I want everyone to see my wonderful, beautiful family and my stunning daughters.' She reached over to touch Sienna's face tenderly. 'I've asked Quinn to come too. She's got a shoot earlier in the day, but she'll come straight on after that. We're all going over to the Randolph in the afternoon to get ready.'

'Isn't it on a Thursday?' asked Sienna.

'Yes, why?'

'Won't we be at school?'

Helena laughed. 'Oh, don't worry about that. I'll just write you a little note. They'll understand, I'm sure.'

Corin frowned. 'Helena . . .'

'What's the matter?'

'You really can't do things like that. The girls can come along to the hotel after school's finished for the day. It's only half-past three, after all.'

Helena rolled her eyes. 'You're such a stuffed shirt sometimes, Corin. What does a half-day off matter?'

He looked at her. 'Helena, darling . . .'

She sighed. 'Oh, all right, all right. At least I won't have to argue with the headmistress about it. We'll book a taxi to bring the girls straight to the hotel from school.' Corin kissed her hand.

Sienna shot a delighted look at Lola. 'Cool!'

'I've booked a hairdresser and a couple of make-up people to help us get ready on the day,' Helena said. 'And I thought maybe you'd like to come shopping next week, Sienna, to choose an outfit.'

Sienna beamed. 'Brilliant!'

Lola tried not to feel resentful, but she wished she were going too. Her mother saw her downcast expression. 'We'll go another time,' she said soothingly.

There was a sound like a tinkling wind chime from under the table. 'That's your phone,' Sienna said to Lola.

Lola glanced at Corin. 'Can I take it?'

He nodded. 'We're about finished here. And Lola – I really am very sorry about your disappointment.'

'Thanks.' She got up from the table and flipped open the phone as she headed into the hall.

It was Naiha, and at first Lola couldn't understand what she was saying. 'Slow down!' she said, alarmed. Naiha sounded as though she were absolutely hysterical with tears.

'No . . . Bollywood . . . Dad . . . messed up . . .' Naiha choked between sobs.

'Oh no!'

'Mum said . . . shouldn't be surprised . . . always letting us down . . .'

'Oh, Naiha, I'm so sorry. I thought everything was sorted?'

'Me . . . too . . .' Naiha hiccupped.

'What are you going to do?'

'Mum rang . . . the school . . .' Naiha started crying again and the next few words were completely incomprehensible.

'Miss Bourne said what? What did you say?'

'Animals . . .' Naiha managed. 'I'm coming . . . with you . . .'

Lola felt her heart lift. 'Really? To the animal sanctuary?'

'Yeah.' It was clear Naiha was less than enthusiastic, but Lola was thrilled.

'Thank goodness! I won't be there on my own! I am *so* glad you're coming too!'

'Yeah, well . . . no offence, but,' Naiha blew her nose, 'I'm not.'

Corin was loading the dishwasher when Lola went back into the kitchen, snapping the phone shut. Sienna and Helena were still sitting at the kitchen table, looking at a copy of *Harper's Bazaar*.

'Naiha's lost her work experience placement too,' announced Lola.

Sienna was shocked. 'She's not going to India?'

'No, her dad let her down.'

28

'Oh dear,' said Helena, 'poor thing. That's awful.'

'Is this the father who's a film producer?' asked Corin, closing the dishwasher with a snap.

'Yes, he works in Bollywood,' Lola said, sitting down next to her mother. 'He's a bit flaky. He's always doing things like this. But Naiha totally believed him this time – she was packed and everything.'

'She must be devastated,' said Helena. 'Has the school been able to find her anything instead?'

'Yeah, she's coming to the animal sanctuary with me.'

Helena brightened. 'Oh well, that's nice. At least you'll both be in the same place. You can cheer each other up.'

'Mmm.'

Sienna giggled. 'Sorry,' she said. 'I am really gutted for Naiha, but I just can't see her at an animal sanctuary. Is she absolutely ballistic at the idea?'

'She wasn't pleased,' admitted Lola.

'I bet. Wonder how long she'll last?'

'We're there for the week.'

'Yes,' said Sienna with a knowing look, 'but she's not exactly Miss Quiet, is she? I mean, how long before she blows up at someone?'

Lola felt uncomfortable. 'I'm sure she'll be fine.' Her phone beeped with a text message, closely followed by a second. 'News has got round.' She showed her mother. 'It's Tasha and Alisha.' The messages from her friends were exclaiming over Naiha's bad luck and saying how sorry they were that both she and Lola were going to have to work somewhere really boring.

'Tactful,' commented Corin, reading the messages over his wife's shoulder. 'You might have a more interesting week than they will.'

'I don't think so,' said Lola. 'Tasha's at the BBC and Alisha's at a music studio.'

'So? Bet they end up making the tea all week. That's what you do on work experience.'

Helena looked puzzled. 'Is that what the kids do at your health clubs when they're on work experience?'

Corin backtracked hastily. 'Of course not. They – er – they do all sorts of things.' He grinned. 'It's just that making tea is the one duty that isn't forbidden by Health and Safety.'

'Samir won't be making tea,' put in Sienna. 'He's already been given a schedule. Till, stocktaking, merchandise, all that kind of thing.'

As if on cue, Lola's phone beeped with a message from Samir. 'What's it say?' asked Sienna.

'None of your business.' Lola stood up again. 'I'm going to ring him. See you in a bit.'

'Don't forget to ring Quinn after that!' her mum called after her.

♥

'Naiha texted me,' Samir said, when she rang. 'What happened?'

'Dunno.' Lola flopped down onto her bed. 'Her dad let her down, that's all I know.'

'And she's got to work at the animal place too?'

'Yeah. She's *so* not happy.'

'Are you OK?'

Lola sighed. 'Yeah. I guess so. I've had a bit of time to think about it, you know? Let it sink in. It's only for a week.'

'Yeah – and then we can go do something more fun.'

She tucked her mobile under her ear and reached down to pull off her socks. 'What about this weekend? What are we going to do?'

'What do you want to do?'

Lola wriggled her bare toes in the deep luxurious carpet. 'Can we go somewhere really cool? I dunno. You remember that massive warehouse place that had all those indoor rides and games?'

'The place we went to for Alisha's birthday?'

'Yes, that one. Do you know where it is?'

'No idea. Why don't I text Ali and ask her? I could get my dad to take us. Or my brother.'

'Can we ask Naiha along too?'

Samir hesitated. 'Is she going to be all moody?'

'Well, she is a bit upset . . .'

'I don't want her along if she's just going to grump about all the time. You know what she's like.'

'She's my friend, Sam . . .' Lola made her voice persuasive. 'It'll help cheer her up. Please?'

A sigh came down the phone line. 'Oh, all right. If it means I get to spend time with *you* . . .'

Lola smiled, her cheeks flushing pink. 'You spend loads of time with me.'

'No, I don't, there are always other people around. Tell you what.' Samir brightened up. 'Let's plan to do something after work experience week – just you and me. I know – I'll take you out to dinner.'

'Just me?' Lola felt her stomach flip. She'd never been out to dinner with a boy before – not just the two of them. 'Where?'

'It'll be a surprise.'

She giggled. 'Tell me.'

'No. You'll have to wait and see. And wear something pretty.'

'OK.' Lola twisted a long strand of her blonde hair

around her finger. 'That sounds cool. And if work experience gets really bad, I'll have something to look forward to at the end of the week.'

'Lola, I gotta go. I'll text you later when I've heard from Alisha.'

'OK. Bye, then.'

'Bye,' he said, and the phone clicked off.

Lola sat on the bed and hugged herself. She was so lucky to have Samir as her boyfriend. He was as perfect as perfect could be!

# Chapter 3

## this is nothing like Animal 24:7

'Are those the wellies you wore to Glastonbury?' Naiha asked as the two of them got out of Corin's car on Monday morning.

Lola looked down at her boots, which had a pattern of pink ice-cream cones all over them. 'Yeah. I wanted to wear my Uggs, but Mum said they'd get too dirty. I've got three pairs of socks on so my feet don't get cold.'

The two girls had agreed on their clothing the night before. Lola was wearing a White Stuff shirt over an All Saints vest, and a pale pink Top Shop cardigan, whilst her legs were clad in skinny jeans, held up by a studded belt. Naiha was also wearing skinny jeans along with a French Connection stretchy top and a short-sleeved cashmere jumper in black. On her feet she had ankle-high suede boots.

Naiha said critically, 'We look good.'

Corin, looking out of the window, snorted. 'You're going to freeze. I told you to pick up a coat, Lola. It is February, you know.'

Lola flapped a manicured hand at him. 'Sorry, I forgot. We'll be fine.'

Her stepfather rolled his eyes, amused. 'Fashion comes first, I know! Just don't blame me if you come home with frostbite. Have a good day, you two!' He revved the car and drove away.

As the two girls walked up to the gates, Lola shivered slightly. It *was* pretty cold today and the wind was chilly. Never mind, the animals must be in heated buildings, mustn't they? So it wouldn't matter that she hadn't brought a coat. And she did look nice, she knew that. She wanted to make a good impression. Maybe if the managers liked her, she wouldn't have to do anything too gross.

They shut the gate carefully behind them. 'Is this really it?' Naiha asked, dismayed.

Lola looked around. The place looked like a travellers' camp. To her right was a small field with some sheep and a goat; to her left, a row of ramshackle buildings, some of them little more than sheds. A caravan stood just behind them, and although there was a traditional 'house' a little further up, it was hard to see it behind all the sheds and cabins. The noise of dogs barking reached the girls' ears.

Naiha paled under her dark skin. 'Oh my God, this place is, like, a dump.'

Lola stared. 'This can't be it.'

'The sign on the gate said Parchester Animal Sanctuary.'

'But where are the buildings? I mean . . .' Lola felt panicked. 'This is nothing like *Animal 24:7*.'

A slim girl with frizzy blonde hair came out of a shed to their left and caught sight of them. 'You all right?' she called.

'We're here on work experience,' Lola said, annoyed that her voice sounded shaky.

The girl nodded. 'Oh, right. Go up to the office, then.' She turned away.

'Where's that?' Lola called after her.

The girl looked vaguely surprised. 'Up there.' She pointed.

Lola and Naiha could just make out a small shed with a corrugated roof. 'She can't mean that one,' muttered Naiha.

'We'll have to go and see.' Lola wanted nothing more than to turn round and go straight back out of the gates. She could ring Corin, couldn't she? Tell him – tell him they'd made a mistake, that the sanctuary

36

wasn't expecting them after all, they'd have to go home.
But it would be a lie, wouldn't it? And she'd get found
out . . . Lola took a breath. No, they had to go on with
it. By the way Naiha was hesitating next to her, she
knew her friend felt the same reluctance. 'Come on,'
she said. 'At least we're in it together.'

Naiha sighed. 'I guess so.'

'And at least we had a great weekend. Just keep
thinking about that instead.'

Her friend brightened. 'Yeah. The Warehouse was
*awesome*.'

Trying to avoid the potholes, they headed up the
driveway, past the sheep and goat, and the large
barn-like building. 'My boots are going to be ruined,'
groaned Naiha. Lola was thankful she was at least
wearing wellies, but she was definitely wishing she'd
followed Corin's advice and brought a coat. The
February wind was bitingly cold.

A small sign saying RECEPTION was stuck in the
corner of the corrugated shed's window. Lola knocked
hesitantly on the door.

'Come in!' called a man's voice.

The door opened outwards, and a large white
cat stood on the threshold, glaring at them. 'Don't
mind Chalky,' came the voice. 'He thinks he owns
this place.'

Lola and Naiha stared at the cat, and the cat stared back. 'We've got a cat at home,' said Naiha, reaching out to him hopefully. 'She's really friendly.'

Chalky bared his teeth, and Naiha snatched her hand back. Lola made a small yelping noise of fright.

'Chalky isn't,' said the man. 'He doesn't like being stroked, sorry.' Dark-haired and wearing glasses, he was sitting the other side of a small desk piled high with paperwork and a laptop computer. 'Just go round him.'

Lola and Naiha sidled past the mean-looking cat, casting nervous looks at him. Chalky watched them squeeze into the office, then leaped onto the desk and began to wash himself. The shed was crammed with files, boxes, dog collars, several old towels, two chairs with the stuffing sticking out and all sorts of things Lola didn't recognize. There were shelves all around the room, overflowing with stuff. It was cold in here too.

'You must be Lola and Naiha, right?' asked the man. They nodded. 'Nice to meet you. I'm Dan Harper, and I manage the sanctuary. You'll see me around but I mostly handle the paperwork. If you need anything, I'm usually in here. Have a seat.' Lola and Naiha perched on the same chair. Lola tried not to touch anything. *I'm going to get cat and dog hairs all over my cardigan*, she thought. She felt petrified. What if all the animals were as unfriendly as Chalky? She hadn't even thought that she might end up getting bitten! What could you catch from animals? Her mind raced. Was it rabies? Or that thing rabbits died of – mixosomething? Could humans get it?

'Have you brought coats?' Dan broke into her thoughts. They shook their heads. He looked surprised 'You're going to get very cold.'

'We'll be fine,' replied Naiha. Lola could see the goosebumps on her wrists.

'Yeah,' she echoed, because Dan was looking expectantly at her. 'We'll be fine, honestly.' She clasped her freezing hands together. 'We – we don't feel the cold.'

The corners of Dan's mouth twitched as though he were amused. 'Well, if you change your mind, there are some fleeces hanging on the back of the door.' He indicated the mixture of navy, green and black jumpers. 'Help yourself.'

Lola, who was closest to the door, wrinkled her nose. The fleeces smelled of mud and cat fur. 'No, it's all right, thank you.'

Dan shrugged. 'It's up to you. But you might want

to come in old clothes tomorrow. You don't want to worry about getting smart stuff dirty.'

Lola's heart sank. *Old clothes?* She didn't have any old clothes! Anything she didn't like, or that didn't fit, or had holes in, was simply taken to the charity shop. Helena and Corin both agreed that unwanted clothes should be given to people who might need them. Why would anyone keep *old clothes*, for goodness' sake? One sideways glance at Naiha suggested that she felt the same way. Lola bit her lip in an effort to stop it wobbling. This place was just too strange. How was she going to be able to cope with a whole week here?

Naiha, usually outspoken and unfazed by anything, seemed to have frozen to the spot.

Dan looked curiously from one to the other and then shrugged. 'Well, we'd better get on with things, hadn't we?' He smiled. 'You probably want to know what you're doing today. First of all I have to go through some Health and Safety policies with you, and then I'll take you over to Maggie. She's in charge of all the cats, and she'll show you what to do.'

Lola felt Naiha relax a little. Naiha would be all right with cats – apart from Chalky, of course, who was still washing himself on the desk. And Lola liked Naiha's cat. Shandi was friendly and playful and didn't dig her claws in when you stroked her. But Lola hadn't really met any other cats. How many were there? A few? Twenty, maybe?

The Health and Safety stuff seemed to take an age. Lola found her mind wandering again. How many different animals did they have in this place altogether? Cats and dogs, of course, and she'd seen a sheep and a goat on the way in. Why would you have sheep and goats in a sanctuary? Shouldn't they be out in fields? And why – the burning question – *why* did it look nothing like the RSPCA on television?

Dan noticed she wasn't listening. 'Lola, this might seem boring to you, but it's important.'

Lola flushed. 'Sorry.'

Naiha put her hand on top of Lola's and dug her nails in. Lola knew what that meant. Naiha was signalling *Oh my God I can't believe we have to listen to all of this it's so boring and I'm freezing*. She gripped Naiha's hand back. At least her best friend was with her. At least she didn't have to go through this on her own.

By the time Dan had finished explaining everything, and they'd signed the necessary paperwork, Lola was so cold she thought she might have frozen to Naiha and the chair. She was relieved when Dan said he would show them around the place, though when he opened the door and let in a blast of cold air, she was less than thrilled. 'Have a fleece,' Dan said mildly.

Lola glanced at Naiha. *I really don't want to, she was thinking, because I'll look like a tramp, but I am completely freezing and if Naiha does then I will too.* Naiha looked hard at her. Then her shoulders slumped and she reached for a navy fleece. Lola wrapped herself in a dark green one and breathed out. It smelled awful, but it was warm.

'You can leave your bags in here,' Dan said. 'They'll be quite safe.'

There was no lock on the door that Lola could see. She hesitated. As well as her purse and her phone, she also had her camera with her, in case there were opportunities to take photos of cute animals. How safe would her things be?

'This way,' said Dan cheerfully, and set off round the back of the shed. Lola glanced at Naiha, and the two of them reluctantly put their bags into a gap on a shelf before following Dan out.

'The dogs are over here, we've got seventy at the moment.'

'*Seventy?*' whispered Naiha to Lola in shock. 'Did he say *seventy?*'

'Where do they all come from?' Lola wondered out loud.

Dan heard her. 'From everywhere in the county. Anyone who doesn't want their dog any more, or who finds a dog wandering the streets, or one that's been taken away from its owners because of ill-treatment – they all end up here.'

'But *seventy?*' asked Naiha. 'That's loads.'

'What do you do with them all?' asked Lola, plunging her hands into the fleece pockets before withdrawing them hastily. What was that sticky stuff in the right-hand one? *Eurgh* – now she had it stuck under her nails! Surreptitiously, she picked at it.

'What do you mean?' asked Dan. 'We look after them, that's what we do. We feed them, walk them, make sure they have their vaccinations. Treat them if they're ill. You know, like they're our pets.' He turned to look at the two of them. 'You said you had a cat at home?'

'Well, yeah,' admitted Naiha, 'but I don't really do much of the looking after.'

'What about you, Lola? Do you have pets?'

She shook her head. 'We've never had anything.'

Dan raised his eyebrows. 'So you don't have much experience of animals, then?'

'Not really.' Lola felt embarrassed. Until now, she'd only thought about how disappointed she was to be working here. It hadn't occurred to her that the

manager of the sanctuary might be disappointed in
the girls he'd been sent. 'Um . . . this wasn't our first
choice for work experience.'

'Ah, I see.' Dan nodded, as though he understood.
Then he smiled. 'Never mind, I'm sure you'll get used
to us. Everyone does.'

Lola tried to smile back, but she found it hard
to believe him. The thought of dealing with seventy
dogs was scarier than anything she could imagine!
Plus, the noise was beginning to get on her nerves.
There was something about a dog's bark that went
right through her, and being so close to so many
yapping and woofing animals made her jittery.

'So we take care of the animals,' Dan continued,
'until they're rehomed. A lot of people come looking
for a new family pet. That's mainly what we do here
– take in unwanted animals and make them wanted
again.' He smiled again as his eyes landed on an area
of outside pens. 'That's the best part of the job,' he
said softly. 'Seeing an animal go off happy with a
new family.'

'What's the worst?' asked Lola, eyeing a small brown
and white dog who was looking wistfully up at her
from its cage. That one looked quite sweet, didn't it?
Maybe she could ask if she could just look after the
smaller ones . . .

Dan gave a sigh. 'The death of an animal. Always hard.'

'Do you . . .' Lola hesitated. 'Do you – put them down? If you've got too many, I mean.'

'No,' said Dan fiercely. 'Never. An animal is only ever put to sleep if it's suffering too much. No other reason.'

The girls followed Dan across the yard, and Naiha threw Lola a look. Lola shrugged helplessly.

'Ah,' said Dan as they rounded a corner, 'this is Harry.'

Harry was carefully muzzling a large dog in a pen to their left. He was about their own age, with a shock of mid-brown hair that curled so much it looked like it had never been brushed. He had blue eyes bordered by dark lashes, and his face was spattered with freckles. Two or three dark smudges covered most of one cheek and his hands were filthy. He looked more like a gardener or a chimney sweep than an animal worker. However, the way he handled the dog suggested he knew exactly what he was doing. His fingers worked deftly to secure the buckles, and he kept up a low murmur all the time. The dog stood patiently, only its ear twitching. Once he had finished, Harry looked up and his gaze passed over Lola and Naiha with a complete lack of interest. 'Hi.'

'Hi,' said Naiha as Lola was opening her mouth. 'You all right?'

Harry looked faintly puzzled. 'Yeah.' He bent to the dog again, patting it gently.

'What's that for?' asked Naiha, nodding towards the muzzle.

Harry threw a glance at Dan. 'It's a muzzle,' he said simply.

'Yes, but what does it do?'

Harry stared at her.

Lola broke in hastily. 'It's to stop them biting, right?' She kept her distance. Dogs that needed muzzles were scary!

'Harry's an expert with our stronger dogs,' Dan said. 'He can handle them better than anyone.'

Lola saw Harry's face redden at the praise before he bent over the dog again.

'This is Lola and Naiha,' said Dan. 'They're here for the week on work experience.'

Harry nodded. 'OK.' Then he clipped a lead to the dog's collar. 'I've got to go.' He set off past the three of them without a backward glance, the dog trotting obediently by his side.

'That dog will never be rehomed,' Dan said sadly. 'He was owned by a burglar and taught to attack.'

Lola's eyes grew wide and she took an involuntary

step back. 'To *attack*?' she repeated. 'You mean – biting and everything? People actually *teach* their dogs to do that?'

'Sometimes,' replied Dan. 'Very sad. Awful what people do to their animals. We can't ever let him go to a new family, it's not safe.'

'Then why don't you put him down?' asked Naiha bluntly.

'Because it's not his fault and he's not ill,' said Dan. 'Now, over here . . .'

The two girls followed him, both casting glances over their shoulders to the disappearing Harry. 'What a *mess*!' whispered Naiha. 'Did you see his hands? And his hair! Do you think he even knows what a brush is?'

Lola had been wondering how Harry had learned to deal with rough dogs, but Naiha's words made her look around in embarrassment. 'Ssh, Naiha, Dan will hear you!'

'Wonder what school he goes to,' went on Naiha. 'I mean, he's not anyone *we* know . . .'

'This is the cat area,' Dan said.

Lola and Naiha clapped their hands to their noses. 'What is that *smell*?'

'They need cleaning out,' came a deep female voice. 'Not done it yet.'

'This is Maggie,' Dan told them. 'She's in charge of our one hundred and twenty cats.'

*One hundred and twenty?* Lola felt faint. Everywhere she looked, there were cats. Tortoiseshell, black and white, tabby, Siamese . . . Lola had never seen so many all in one place.

Maggie reached out to shake hands. The girls had no choice. Maggie's hand felt rough, and her fingernails were black with dirt. 'Nice to meet you,' she said, beaming. Her long black hair was scraped back into an untidy plait, and she wore a thick green coat which had seen better days. 'But I think Ruth needs more help with the rabbits today, since Kevin called in sick.'

'You have one hundred and twenty cats?' Naiha said, horrified, her hand still clamped to her nose.

Maggie smiled, her eyes crinkling at the corners. 'I know. Wonderful, isn't it? How lucky am I to spend all day with these beautiful creatures?'

Naiha gave a cough that could have been a snort. Lola didn't know what to say. Yes, one cat might be lovely, but a hundred and twenty? And the smell was overpowering . . .

'Can you manage today?' Dan asked Maggie. 'If I take the girls over to Ruth?'

She nodded. 'No problem. I'll have them tomorrow instead, if that's all right.'

Dan turned to Lola and Naiha. 'Come on, then. The rabbits are in that big building you saw on your way in.'

'How many people have you got working here?' asked Naiha casually as they left Maggie and the cats. Lola shot her a curious look. 'I mean, is there anyone else our age?'

Lola realized what her friend meant and stifled a smile. Surely Naiha didn't think they'd be working with any fit boys, did she?

'Only Harry,' said Dan, his attention caught by a small hole in the wire fence. 'Must get that fixed before Benjy gets out.'

Naiha sighed. Lola could tell what she was thinking. Working in this smelly place and not even a boy to drool over! Her thoughts turned to Samir. What kind of a morning was he having? Working in a shop wouldn't usually be top of her list, but at that moment she'd have gladly swapped places with him.

'*Ew!*' Naiha stopped suddenly. 'What the – what is *that*?' She clutched Lola's arm and lifted her boot slightly. A large dark patch clung to the side of it. Naiha groaned. 'I don't believe it. That is just *gross*.'

Dan turned to look. 'Oh, sorry. You've got to look

where you're going round here. It'll wash off all right, I expect.'

'Wash?' Naiha glared at her boot. 'This is *suede*.'

'Mm?' Dan's attention was already on something else. 'Must get that hinge looked at. Here we are.'

Lola and Naiha picked their way cautiously over, scanning the ground for any more dogs' mess. Lola was doubly relieved she was wearing her wellies.

The rabbit building was enormous and filled with hutches and wire runs. Like the cat building, there were animals everywhere. Lola felt slightly better, though – at least rabbits were easier to handle, right? And there were some really cute ones with fluffy fur. 'How many rabbits have you got at the moment?' she asked.

'Seventy-three,' answered a young woman in denim dungarees and a thick roll-neck jumper. Lola realized she was the girl they'd seen on their arrival, who had pointed them in the direction of the office.

'This is Ruth,' Dan told them. 'These are the work experience girls, Lola and Naiha. Ruth's been working here for five years now.'

Lola was surprised. Ruth didn't look that much older than the two of them. She had short bleached-blonde hair that stuck out from her head like a dandelion clock. Could she be nineteen? Twenty?

How come she'd been working here for so long?

Ruth saw Lola's surprise. Her mouth twisted slightly. 'I came here for work experience too. Never left.'

'Oh!' Lola was taken aback. Ruth was quite pretty – and still young. Why did she want to work here all the time?

Ruth reached for a couple of pairs of gloves and handed them to the girls. 'Here you go. You'll need these.'

'I'll leave them to you,' Dan said. 'Don't forget to take your morning break, girls.'

'OK,' said Ruth. 'As you can see, there are runs and hutches on two levels. They all need cleaning out today. Have either of you ever cleaned out a hutch or a cage before?'

They shook their heads. Ruth looked surprised. 'Really? You never had a rabbit as a pet when you were little? Or a guinea pig, or a hamster maybe?'

'Nothing,' said Lola.

'I've got a cat,' said Naiha, for what seemed like the fifteenth time, 'but I don't clean the litter tray, Mum does that.'

'OK, well, you'll soon get the hang of it. Rabbits are easy to clean out.' Ruth looked down. 'Oh. What was your name again?'

'Naiha.'

'Nye-hah?' Ruth tried, puzzled.

'No, Naiha. Like a horse neigh. Neigh-a.'

'Sorry. I'll try to get it right. Um, did you bring any wellies? Only I'm afraid your suede boots are going to get really dirty.'

Naiha's face was like thunder. 'They already are. I trod in some mess on the way in here.'

'Oh, sorry about that. But I guess if they're already dirty . . .' Ruth tried to be sympathetic. 'I mean, you've got to clean them later anyway, haven't you?' She saw Naiha's expression. 'Oh, I didn't mean . . . um, haven't you got any wellies?'

'She's got some at home,' Lola interrupted on Naiha's behalf. 'She'll wear them tomorrow.'

Ruth looked sympathetic. 'Didn't your school tell you what to wear?'

'We're not meant to be here,' explained Lola. 'This was a last-minute thing.'

'Oh.' Ruth was taken aback. 'Oh, I see – what were you meant to be doing, then?'

'I was meant to be working at Mulberry,' Lola said. She could hear her own voice wobble.

'Where?'

'Mulberry. You know, the fashion label?'

'Oh, right.' Ruth shrugged. 'Sorry, I don't really keep up with fashion.'

*How could anyone not have heard of Mulberry?* Lola wondered in amazement.

'I was meant to be working in India with my dad,' said Naiha fiercely. 'He's a film director.'

'Wow. So what happened?'

Naiha's lips clamped together again.

'Bit of a mix-up,' said Lola, but she didn't want to say any more. After all, they didn't really know Ruth, and Naiha wouldn't thank her for spilling her family's problems to a stranger. She was also afraid she might get upset if she told Ruth about missing out on the week in London, and that would be embarrassing.

Ruth looked from one to the other. 'Oooo-kay. Well, that's a shame, but I'm sure you'll love it here.'

*I don't think so,* Lola said to herself.

'And we've got a lot to get through, so let's get started.' Ruth began by pointing out where the buckets, disinfectant, dustpans and brushes were, along with the large room out the back where the hay, sawdust and newspaper lived. 'Just watch out for rats,' she said matter-of-factly. 'We do our best to keep them down, but they like the warmth and the fact there's food available.'

'Rats?' Naiha squeaked, looking around wildly.

Ruth laughed. 'Don't worry, they're not dangerous

or anything. Just let me or Dan know if you see one – we have to act fast.'

Lola clenched her fists inside her thick gardening gloves, feeling the sticky substance still on her fingers. This was like her worst nightmare come true! Cleaning out rabbit hutches! Watching for rats! Working with someone who'd never heard of *Mulberry*, for goodness' sake!

It was unpleasant work. The rabbit runs were lined with newspaper, on which was spread sawdust. Lola and Naiha had to roll up the paper with the sawdust inside and dump it into a large wheelbarrow. The paper was soggy with urine, and the sawdust thick with droppings. Lola was thankful she was wearing gloves, but she still did her best not to touch the wet patches. Naiha, her eyes glued to the droppings on the floor to avoid stepping in them, also picked up the paper very gingerly.

'No need to be delicate about it,' Ruth said, watching them. 'We've got twenty-five to clean out, so you can't take all day.'

Naiha's expression showed just what she thought of that!

After the paper had been taken up, the hay had to be removed from the hutch and the whole lot had to be mopped with animal-friendly disinfectant. 'We have so many rabbits here,' Ruth said, cradling a rabbit with long floppy ears in her lap, 'we can't take risks with infection or disease. We need them to be as healthy as possible, don't we, Holly?'

It took a moment for Lola to realize she was talking to the rabbit. 'What happens if they're not healthy?' she asked, to take her mind off the work.

'Well, for a start, no one will want them. People come in here all the time looking for a pet, usually for their kids. No one wants an ill rabbit. And if one gets ill, it spreads really quickly. It can cost a fortune in vet's bills.'

'Don't the vets treat them for free?' asked Lola, trying to wipe a sticky dropping off her glove.

Ruth let out a sarcastic laugh. 'Free? No, why should they?'

'I thought, because it's a sanctuary . . . I mean, it's a charity, isn't it?'

'Yeah, but we still have to pay the vet, just like everyone else.' Ruth pointed. 'You've missed a bit, Naiha. Make sure you get right into the corners.' Naiha glowered at the mop.

Once the floor of the run was mopped, they had to dry it with a towel. Then they had to put down new newspaper and spread fresh sawdust on top. Finally, there was new hay to go in the hutch and clean water in the bottle.

Lola wiped her forehead with her arm, wishing she'd tied her hair back from her face. Every time she leaned forward, the long blonde strands fell in front of her eyes. Her back was starting to ache a bit too, from all the bending down. And she still had sticky fingernails inside her glove.

'One down,' said Ruth, grinning, 'twenty-four to go!'

Naiha looked like she was about to explode, but her lips were pressed tightly together. Lola shot her an anxious glance. It would be awful if Naiha made a scene on their very first morning! She didn't want to work here, but it would be doubly bad if she didn't have Naiha to keep her company. She fervently hoped that Naiha would calm down a bit.

'And now you know how to do it, you should be able to work separately,' Ruth added. 'It'll be faster that way and you won't get under each other's feet.'

Lola thought of the offices at Mulberry, which in her mind were all shiny and warm and clean, and then she looked at the urine-soaked newspaper and the brown rabbit droppings everywhere, and she wanted to cry.

# Chapter 4

## I never realized rabbits were so dangerous

'How many is that?' asked Naiha in exhaustion, lifting two large black rabbits back into their clean pen.

'Twelve,' replied Ruth. 'Only thirteen to go.'

'Twelve?' repeated Naiha in amazement. 'No, surely we have to have done more than that.'

Lola's back ached, and her knees felt stiff. She was even more baffled that Ruth chose to do this every week. *When there are so many other nice jobs out there*, she thought to herself, *why would anyone do this?*

'Don't worry,' said Ruth, 'when you do it again on Thursday you'll be a lot faster.'

'What are you talking about?'

'Well, the rabbits have to be cleaned out twice a week,' Ruth said in a reasonable tone of voice. 'They can't do it themselves.'

'But *we* won't have to do it again,' said Naiha. 'I mean, we've done it once already.'

'Yes,' said Ruth patiently, 'and it'll have to be done again.'

Naiha scowled. 'Can't someone else do it?'

'Why should they?' asked Ruth lightly. 'You're here on work experience, aren't you? Kevin's usually in with me, and sometimes one or two of the others lend a hand, but we don't just sit around, you know. If you're here, you work like the rest of us.' She shrugged with a smile and said, 'That's the point of work experience, right?'

Naiha opened her mouth to reply but at that moment, Harry came into the barn, carrying a drill. She shut her mouth again, casting a curious look in his direction.

Harry glanced over at the two of them but he didn't smile. 'Hi, Harry,' Lola said, but there was no response. Maybe he hadn't heard, so she said it louder. Harry simply grunted. Lola felt hurt. It didn't take much to be nice, did it? Did Harry dislike them? Why?

'Over here, Harry,' said Ruth. She indicated an empty hutch. 'The door's hanging off, think one of the hinges has gone.'

Harry nodded and knelt down on the floor. As she worked, Lola watched him out of the corner of her eye. Once he had examined the hutch, he carefully unscrewed the hinges with the drill and laid it on the floor. Then he reached into his pocket and pulled out a collection of metalwork. Lola couldn't see what it was, but Harry picked through the handful and selected a couple of small items. Then he began drilling new holes in the door and reattaching the hinge. *Wow*, she thought. *I wouldn't have the faintest idea how to mend something like that. He looks like he's been doing it for years.* Despite herself, she was impressed.

Lola coughed and rubbed her hands together noisily, but Harry didn't seem to notice. He was completely absorbed in his task; it was as though he were alone. His hair was slightly too long at the back, but what had been trimmed had been done unevenly. She wondered if Harry had cut it himself. There was a dirty smudge just in front of his left ear, and his hands and fingernails were as black as Maggie's.

The door suddenly slipped on its hinges and Harry swore, glancing at his thumb and then sucking it. 'Are you all right?' Lola asked.

He didn't even bother to turn round. 'Yeah, fine.' After a moment, he went back to his task.

Lola continued her cleaning, but she felt puzzled. Why was he so determined to be unfriendly? She wasn't used to being ignored, particularly by boys.

Had she and Naiha done something to annoy him without knowing? Maybe she should ask him? Thinking hard, she pushed her mop into the corners of the hutch, making it wobble.

Harry looked round. 'Don't do that,' he said. 'Otherwise I'll have to mend that one too.'

Lola quickly turned, pushing her hair back from her face again. 'Sorry,' she said, with her warmest smile. 'I was miles away.' She gave a laugh. 'I'm not used to clearing up poo, you see.'

'No,' said Harry to his hutch. 'I can see that.'

Lola's face flushed. She pressed her lips together and concentrated on her mopping. So much for trying to be nice. Maybe it would be best just to keep away from Harry.

'Ouch!' cried Naiha suddenly. She dropped the rabbit she was holding, and it fell to the ground, scurrying into its clean hutch. 'It bit me!'

'Don't drop them,' said Ruth sternly. 'Don't ever drop an animal. It can break a leg.'

'But it bit me! Right through my glove!' Naiha pulled it off and cradled her hand. 'God!'

'Let me look.' Ruth reached out. 'It's fine, it didn't even break the skin.' Then she turned her attention to the rabbit. 'Come out, Snowball, come on. Let me look at you.' Carefully, she picked up the rabbit and examined its legs. 'Does that hurt? No? Good girl, it's all right.' She turned crossly to Naiha. 'She was frightened. You must have handled her roughly.'

'I just picked it up.' Naiha was irritated. 'Just like I picked up all the others, like you showed me.'

'Well, she doesn't bite normally,' snapped Ruth. 'So you must have done something to hurt her.'

Lola watched, feeling nervous. She could tell her friend's temper was rising again. *Don't blow up*, she thought helplessly. *Keep it together, Naiha!* Glancing across at Harry, she saw him staring at Naiha, frowning. Then he shook his head and turned back to his work. For some reason this made her irritated. *Can't he see she's upset?* she thought.

'Look.' Naiha was holding out her hand for Lola to inspect. 'See what it did?' There was a small red mark at the base of her thumb. It didn't look that serious to Lola, but she knew she couldn't say that.

'Are you OK? I guess it was a bit out of the blue.'

'Yeah.' Naiha was calming down. 'I mean, I was just moving it across, and wham!' She shook her hand ruefully. 'It's got really sharp teeth.'

'You poor thing.' Lola knew that Harry was scoffing from the corner, but she couldn't let down her friend. 'Let me move the next couple across for you.'

'Thanks,' said Naiha. Her voice was returning to its normal pitch. 'I'm just a bit – you know, shaken up. I mean, you know, it could have hit an *artery* or something. I never realized rabbits were so dangerous.'

Lola was thankful that Ruth had gone to the back of the building and didn't hear this. It was embarrassing enough that Harry had let out a snort at Naiha's words. Why did Naiha have to go so over the top about things? She'd had a little nip – surely she'd had worse from her own cat before now? But Lola knew Naiha would go ballistic if she even suggested such a thing, so she just made soothing noises and muttered about getting Corin to buy them some extra-tough gloves for the next day.

After that, things went more smoothly for a while. Lola found that if she didn't really think about what she was doing, it was a bit easier. Harry finished mending the hutch and disappeared again. Lola reached into the next run to lift a rabbit out so she could clean. The rabbit huddled at the back of the run, squeaking slightly. 'I'm not going to hurt you,' Lola told it. 'Come on.' The rabbit shuddered. Lola frowned. That was a bit odd, wasn't it? Did rabbits get cold? Was it shivering?

She called to Ruth. 'Can you come here for a moment? I think there's something wrong with this one.'

Ruth put down her bucket and joined her. 'Which one?'

Lola pointed. 'It's sort of shivering.'

'That's Zippy. She's a bit nervous of people. But she's got really long fur, she shouldn't be cold.'

They stared down at the rabbit, which stared back. 'She looks all right to me,' said Ruth finally. 'Let's get her out.'

Had she imagined it? Lola shook her head. All this bending over and clearing up mess in the cold – she must be getting a bit light-headed.

Ruth carefully checked over the rabbit. 'Can't see anything wrong.' She handed Zippy to Lola. 'Just keep an eye on her.'

Lola cleaned out Zippy's cage, her back aching. *I wonder what Sienna's doing?* she suddenly thought. When Lola had left with Corin this morning, Sienna had still been in bed. Lola thought long-ingly of her nice warm bed, and of other pupils on half term who didn't have to do this stupid work experience. And then she thought about Mulberry, and her eyes filled with tears. Quinn had been so sweet about the whole let-down, even texting her this morning to wish her good luck. Lola was doubly disappointed about not being able to stay with her sister in London. Absentmindedly, she picked up Zippy to put her back into the cage – and the rabbit shuddered in her hands.

'Ruth! She did it again!'

This time there was no mistake. Ruth saw Zippy give another shudder, and her face fell. 'Oh dear. Looks like a chill. Quick, give her here. We need to get her to the vet straight away.' She tucked Zippy into her jacket. The rabbit looked up at her pitifully.

Lola felt something in her constrict. *Poor little thing! It looked so helpless and vulnerable.* 'Will she be all right?'

Ruth's lips pressed tightly together for a moment. 'I don't know. Chills are bad – if that's what it is. Back in a minute.'

Lola watched Ruth carry Zippy quickly out of the barn. 'I hope it's OK.'

Naiha blew out her cheeks. 'Well, if it isn't, it's not like they haven't got lots more.'

Lola opened her mouth to tell Naiha she was being spiteful. It wasn't nice to think of a little thing like that in pain or distress. But she remembered the bite Naiha had had, and it didn't seem the time to disagree with her friend. Sighing, she got back to work.

♥

Lola was thankful when lunch time came around. Everything ached and she knew her hands smelled of rabbit urine, even though she'd been wearing thick gloves. The toilets at the sanctuary were basic and there didn't seem to be very much hot water, so she couldn't even be sure her hands were clean after washing. She wished she'd brought one of the antibacterial hand gels her mother was obsessed with.

'Did you girls bring sandwiches?' asked Dan as they picked up their bags from the office. They shook their heads. 'Well, there's a newsagent at the end of the drive – turn left at the bottom, it's about five minutes' walk. They sell sandwiches and drinks and stuff.' He smiled. 'I know you've had a busy morning, so make sure you have a sit down and a rest. Take a full hour so that you're ready to get back to work this afternoon.'

Naiha raised her eyebrows at Lola, and Lola knew what she was thinking. *Sit down and rest where?*

'What are you doing?' asked Lola as her friend unzipped her fleece. 'It's freezing outside.'

Naiha's expression was obstinate. 'I'm not walking

around town with this thing on. Can you imagine if someone saw me?'

Lola hesitated. Naiha was right. The two girls were normally so fashionably dressed. They took pride in their appearance – unlike, it would appear, the people who worked at the sanctuary. What if they met someone they knew? Everyone in their year at school was on work experience, but there were others. Friends from other year groups, other schools. It would be so embarrassing. Reluctantly, her hand went to her zip. *But it's so cold outside!* whispered the voice in her head. *It's winter, for goodness' sake! Is it really worth catching hypothermia for the sake of a smelly old fleece?* She took a breath. 'I'm keeping it on.'

Naiha looked astounded. 'Well, if you *want* to be seen like that . . .' She left the sentence hanging and pushed open the office door.

Lola threw Dan a nervous glance, but he was staring hard at his laptop screen. If there was a tiny smirk at the corner of his mouth, she must have imagined it, she thought. Clutching her favourite Mulberry bag, she followed Naiha out of the office.

Naiha was checking Facebook on her phone. '*Everyone* else is bragging about how brilliant their work experience is. I can't believe we're here for a whole week. It's only been one morning and already

I feel like I'm going to die from the cold and the work. Why do they *do* it?'

'I don't know. I've been wondering the same thing. Someone has to, I guess. What would happen to all those animals otherwise?' Lola felt reluctant to dig out her own mobile and read the raving messages.

'There's the RSPCA, isn't there? And the Cats Protection League, and that Battersea place. They get smart uniforms and posh offices, I bet. None of this . . .' Naiha swept out an arm, 'this rubbish heap stuff. And they can't even give us lunch! Mind you, not sure I'd eat anything from here anyway, I might catch something.'

'Ssh, someone might hear you.'

'I don't care if they do. You can't possibly *like* it here, Lola.'

Lola dropped her voice. 'I don't. But moaning about it isn't going to make things better, is it?'

Naiha's face brightened. 'I'm calling the school. They should sort this out.'

'Call the school? What for? They won't be able to do anything – it's half term, remember?'

Naiha dialled. 'The teachers will be there, bet you anything.'

'No, they won't – it's a holiday.'

'Don't you remember Mr Kilworth going on about

how he always seemed to spend his holidays in school doing displays and stuff?'

'He's a workaholic. Nobody else does that. Miss Sherlock's always going off to China and Japan and places like that.'

'Hello?' Naiha spoke confidently into the phone. 'Hi, this is Naiha Masih, I'm on work experience this week? Yeah, that's right. Well, no, there's a problem.' She listened for a moment. 'No, not that kind of problem. It's just that this placement is no good for me and my friend, Lola Cassidy. Can I speak to Miss Bourne?' There was another pause. 'Oh. Well, can you get hold of her? Can I have her number then? Oh, for goodness' sake! Yes, yes, all right, I get it. Yeah, bye.' She looked annoyed as she ended the call. 'Miss Bourne isn't in today. That stupid receptionist woman said she couldn't do anything.'

'But there's no point, is there?' Lola asked. 'I mean . . .' She trailed off. It was all so hopeless. She clutched her Mulberry bag even more tightly, trying to imagine herself away from here and sitting in one of those shiny – surely they were shiny? – offices, studying fabrics and patterns. But her imagination, usually to be utterly relied upon, let her down this time. All she could see was a potholed driveway and the creaky gates of the sanctuary. Sighing, she finally pulled out her mobile and began to read the glowing reports from her friends. Even Samir was enthusiastic about his first morning at Next. She gloomily typed a one-sentence reply to him. The others could wait – besides, Naiha was already filling them in on the morning's activities. Lola stuffed her mobile back in her bag and tried not to envy her friends.

The newsagent did indeed sell sandwiches – ham or cheese. 'Oh, for God's sake,' muttered Naiha in disgust. 'There isn't even any salad in with the cheese. Or pickle. It's just slabs of cheese – is there even any margarine?'

Lola was eyeing the sausage rolls in wrappers. 'There's these . . .'

'No way. Do you even *know* what's in sausage rolls?'

In the end, it seemed safest to go for cheese sandwiches, a packet of crisps and a chocolate bar. Lola picked up two bottles of Coke too. 'Here you go.'

'This is full-fat. Haven't they got any Diet? I hate the taste of this one.'

'Nope.'

'Then I'll have water.' Naiha was reluctant to go back outside again too. 'What about a magazine, Lols?' They regarded the covers. 'If you were *her*,' said Naiha, indicating a famous film star on the cover of

*Heat* magazine, 'would you go out in *that*? I mean, nothing matches properly and she hasn't even done her make-up.'

'It says here she was shopping in her local store,' said Lola, picking it up and turning to the article. 'I guess maybe she couldn't be bothered.'

'But she must know photographers are following her around,' said Naiha. 'Who'd have thought her skin was that bad? Look at it – she must be caked in make-up when she does films.'

'I know, it's amazing. Such a difference. But if you have acne, aren't you supposed to let the skin breathe? Putting make-up on makes it worse, doesn't it?'

'I'd risk it,' said Naiha firmly. 'I'd rather hide it under a ton of foundation than have a photo like that on a magazine cover.'

'You buying that or what?' the shopkeeper called from the counter.

'Come on.' Lola grabbed Naiha's arm to take her out of the shop. 'Naiha, your arm is like ice!'

'Of course it is,' snapped her friend. 'I'm freezing my backside off.'

'D'you want to share my fleece?'

'Share it how?'

'I dunno.' Lola started to unzip it. 'We could take turns.'

'No thanks.'

'Naiha, it's just a fleece.' Lola was worried about her friend. 'Come on, no one's going to see.'

Naiha hesitated for a moment, but then shook her head. 'No thanks. Honestly. You keep it. Thanks, though.'

'We need to find somewhere out of the wind. A library or a café or something.' Lola looked hopefully up the street. The only other business in sight was a dry cleaner's.

'This must be the deadest part of Parchester,' said Naiha, rubbing her arms. 'No wonder we never come through this bit of town.'

'Over there.' Lola pointed. There was a bus shelter set back from the kerb, with stone walls and an open door at the front. 'Come on.'

Naiha wrinkled her nose as they went in. 'It stinks.'

'No more than the rabbits.' Lola suddenly found she was starving hungry.

'You know,' Naiha said, biting into her cheese sandwich, 'that we've got to do this essay on work experience after we get back to school?'

'Yeah?'

'Well, I'm going to write the truth – all about how we've been made to work like slaves, doing really disgusting jobs and how it's so – so degrading.'

'They won't care,' said Lola. 'Miss Bourne said she sends people here every year.'

'Well, they shouldn't. It's a pit. It should be shut down. We'll probably get diseases working here.'

'Some people must like it,' mused Lola, a crease appearing between her eyebrows. 'I mean, they wouldn't keep sending students here . . .'

'I can't think of *anyone* who'd like working here,' declared Naiha. 'You'd have to be deranged.'

'Ruth said she first came on work experience, didn't she?' said Lola. 'And she liked it so much she got a job here.'

'Well . . .' Words failed Naiha. Her phone beeped with a text. 'It's Alisha. Oh my God!'

'What is it?'

'Listen to this! *Just got a kiss off Michael Bublé! And he promised to listen to my demo!*'

'*What?* You're joking!'

Naiha was furious. 'Other people have got *brilliant* placements. Like, they're perfectly matched to their interests. Alisha's been singing for years, and she's been trying to get her demo into studios. And here she is practically with a recording contract! You like designing stuff, and I want to be an actress, and we both love modelling – and what are we doing? Cleaning out rabbit hutches!'

Lola tried to be reasonable. 'Miss Bourne said it was the best she could do at short notice . . .'

'I bet she didn't even try to find us something decent. I could have worked backstage at the theatre or something – you could have worked in a photographer's. *I* don't know, there must have been about a billion other possibilities out there. She just looked down her list and went, "The animal sanctuary, no one's working there this week" and bunged us in to save herself more work. Or maybe she wanted to get back at us for messing up at the last minute.'

'Naiha . . .'

'All right, all right.' Naiha shot a glance at her friend. 'You don't have to look at me like that. I'm just having a rant, that's all.'

'I don't think it's helping.'

'Wrong. It makes me feel better to have a good moan.' Naiha gave a sudden grin. 'I guess at least we're in the poo together.'

'Literally.'

'Yeah.' Naiha looked ruefully at her boots. 'Smelly, dirty and freezing cold. Can't get any worse, can it?'

It began to rain.

# Chapter 5

## it's not the sort of thing
## I want to do

Lola was slowly thawing out in a deep hot bath. The bubbles were practically up to the top of the tiled surround, but she didn't care. It was her bubble bath, after all; it was up to her if she wanted to pour in half the bottle. And Philosophy Cinnamon Buns smelled so utterly divine . . .

There was a knock at the door. 'Can I come in?'

It was Sienna. She came in quickly, shutting the door behind her to keep the heat in. 'You OK? You rushed straight up here.'

'I was just really cold.' Lola looked up at her little sister. 'It's absolutely freezing today.'

'I know, I was at the Westford Centre and when we had to go out to the car park, I nearly died.'

'You went to the Westford Centre?'

'Yeah. Not for, like, the whole day – just for lunch and a bit of shopping.'

'Who did you go with?' Lola was instantly envious.

'Mum, of course. But then we met up with Jade and her mum, so we all had lunch together.'

'Where did you eat?' Suddenly Lola wanted to know every single detail – it was almost as though by hearing about her sister's day she could erase her own misery.

'Carluccio's.' Sienna licked her lips. 'I had the ravioli. It was yum.'

Lola tried not to think about her disappointing lunch in the bus shelter.

'Mum insisted on having that disgusting linguine again – you know, the one with squid and weird-looking shellfish in it.' Sienna made a face.

Lola laughed. 'Did you have that gorgeous tiramisu they do?'

'No time,' Sienna said ruefully. 'Mum had booked a manicure and she forgot to tell us until, like, ten minutes before we were due.' She held out her hands so that Lola could see the perfectly polished nails. 'Quite good, don't you think? Not as good as that place we went to in London that time. But they've got loads of cute little things you can have stuck on – like hearts and fruit and flowers. They do spray tans too.'

Lola pulled a face. 'I wouldn't trust someone I didn't know with my tan. Remember what happened to that girl at school?'

'Streaky Bacon?' Sienna giggled. 'She had to stay off for three days in the end, didn't she? How embarrassing!'

'Can't even remember her real name now . . .'

'But the place she went to closed down, didn't it?' asked Sienna. 'Besides, this is a proper one – it's part of a chain, I think.'

'So where did you go after the manicure?' Lola sank back into the bubbles and closed her eyes, inhaling the warm cinnamon scent.

Sienna giggled again. 'You'll never guess.'

'Where?'

'Next!'

Lola opened her eyes. 'Did you see Samir?'

'Yeah. He didn't see us, though. He was by the till, and some guy was explaining stuff to him. Looked like a manager.' Sienna smiled. 'He had this look on his face like he was *really* concentrating.'

'I know that look.' Lola smiled in response. 'He does it in maths.' Unbidden, the image of Samir's concentrating expression was swept aside by Harry's face as he mended the rabbit hutch earlier today. She frowned. Why should she think of him all of a sudden?

Sienna noticed. 'What's up?'

'Oh, nothing. So you didn't go over and say hello then?'

'No. Besides, we were only walking through the menswear section. Mum was on a mission to find this exact pair of tights she wanted. I went, "Look, there's Samir!" and then I had to run to catch up with the others. And this girl gave me the evil eye as I went.'

'What girl?'

'One of the other shop assistants. Really pretty black girl.'

'Why would she give you the evils?'

Sienna shrugged. 'Think it was because I knew Samir. I dunno. Maybe she thought I would interrupt his work or something.'

Lola bit her lip for a moment and then said, 'Was she our age?'

'Hard to tell. Maybe.'

'Oh.' Lola felt a sudden panic. This 'really pretty' black girl, was she on work experience too? Working with Samir? Why would she look like that at Sienna? Unless she fancied Samir . . . Lola shook her head. *Don't be silly*, she told herself. *You're imagining things*. And besides, she trusted Samir, didn't she?

'Lola!'

'What?'

Sienna sighed. 'Never mind, you're not listening.'

'I am! I just . . . Oh, never mind. Sorry, Sienna. I just had a bad day.'

'Don't they have cute rabbits and kittens after all?'

Lola pulled out the bath plug with her toe. 'No. Well, yes, some of them are cute. But the place is awful. I mean, it's like a bunch of sheds, there's no heating, and everything's dirty. And it smells.'

Sienna wrinkled her nose. 'Gross.'

'I know. And I'm there for the whole week,' said Lola gloomily. 'Assuming Naiha doesn't get us thrown out before then.'

Sienna grinned. 'Started already, has she?'

'You have *no* idea. Pass me my towel.'

Sienna reached out for the lilac bath sheet. 'Aren't there *any* good things about working there?'

Lola hesitated. Out of the blue, the image of Harry mending the hutch swam into her head again. 'There's this boy . . .'

Sienna's eyebrows shot up. 'A *boy*? What kind of boy?'

Lola wrapped herself in the towel and stepped carefully out of the bath. 'Oh, just some boy. He's a bit weird, to be honest. Really rude and unfriendly.'

Sienna laughed. 'So why is he a good thing?'

'He isn't, really.' Lola shook her head, clearing the memory. 'Come on, I'm starving.'

♥

Her mother was staring at the phone in the hallway when Lola came down the stairs. 'Oh, hello, darling, nice day?'

'No, not really. Is something wrong?'

'Quinn just called,' said Helena, sounding puzzled. 'She's coming down tomorrow.'

'What, to stay?'

'Yes, she said for a few days.'

Lola smiled. 'That's great! So I'll get to see her after all.'

'Yes . . . She sounded a bit odd. Never mind.' Helena turned to beam at her daughter. 'It'll be lovely to see her, won't it? Now, tell me about your day.'

Lola followed her mother into the kitchen,

where Corin was dishing up some rice. 'It was horrible. I spent the whole day cleaning out rabbits.'

Corin glanced up at her. 'Someone's got to, I suppose.'

'Yes, but I didn't think it would be me. Not on work experience. I mean, it's like Naiha says, we're practically slave labour.'

Corin laughed. 'Don't over-react, Lola. You're there to see what work is like for people in real jobs. They gave you a real job.'

'But it's not the sort of thing *I* want to do,' argued Lola. 'I mean, I'm not going to work in an animal sanctuary when I grow up.'

'You never know where life will take you,' Corin said, sitting down with the rest of them. 'I never thought I'd run health clubs.'

Sienna looked at him. 'What did you want to do?'

He grinned. 'Be an astronaut, of course. Or, failing that, a ninja.' His wife smiled at him indulgently.

Sienna giggled. 'No, seriously?'

'Very seriously – when I was eight. By the time I left school I knew neither of those options would really be possible. So I became a PE teacher.'

'I didn't know that!' Lola was surprised.

'I enjoyed it,' said Corin, 'though I don't think most of the kids did. I used to take them on cross-country runs in the rain.'

'That's just cruel,' commented Sienna. 'PE teachers get off on making people miserable.'

Corin grinned again. 'Nah, that's just an added bonus.'

'Why did you stop being a teacher?' asked Lola.

'Too much paperwork, even in PE,' Corin told her. 'And I got fed up of shouting at the kids who wouldn't behave. So I started working in a gym instead, shouting at the people in my class and filling in more forms.' He laughed. 'Same old, same old.'

Lola's phone rang. She glanced at Corin.

'It'll have to wait,' he said mildly.

The display said it was Samir calling. Lola, biting her lip, hit 'Busy'. She really wanted to talk to him, she suddenly realized – if only to reassure herself that the pretty girl Sienna had seen wasn't actually working in Samir's department. 'Corin,' she said, an idea forming, 'do you think I could swap placements tomorrow? I mean, do you think you could ring the sanctuary and say I'd found somewhere else to work? Like . . . Next, for example?'

He looked amused. 'But you haven't.'

'No, but couldn't you pull a few strings . . . ?'

'Lola,' he said with a sigh, 'you can't just move the world around to suit you. We've talked about this. Helena . . .'

His wife looked sympathetic. 'He's right, darling. We said all of this over the weekend. I'm sorry you're not enjoying it. Just try to think of the weekend. There are only four days to go.'

Lola looked down at her near-empty bowl of rice and pressed her lips together. She should have known not to ask, but she couldn't help herself. The thought of going back to the sanctuary tomorrow was just too depressing for words. Although . . . she kind of wanted to know how that rabbit was doing.

♥

'What girl?' asked Samir, when she rang.

'I don't know. Black and pretty, that's what Sienna said.' Lola tried to sound casual.

'Oh, you mean Safi! Yeah, she's cool.'

Lola's heart sank. 'Is she on work experience too, then?'

'Yeah, from a different school.' Samir began to laugh. 'She's really funny. She went to the Gents' by

82

mistake and this bloke came in and started asking her questions and she tried to pretend he was the one who'd made a mistake. We laughed for about half an hour over that one.'

'Oh. So is she working in your department?'

'Yeah. She was meant to be in Accessories but they swapped her. She said she hates bags and belts and hats anyway. She's hilarious.'

Lola was not feeling reassured. 'There's a boy at my work experience too,' she said, hoping this would alarm Samir.

'Oh yeah?'

'Yes, he's called Harry. He's totally amazing at mending things.'

'Cool.' Samir didn't sound in the least bothered. 'I got your text earlier, sorry you had such a bad time there. But maybe tomorrow will be better, hey?'

'Yeah. But I don't think—'

'Sorry, Lola, I've got to go. My mum's been yelling at me to get downstairs for something. Call you tomorrow, OK?'

'Samir . . .'

'Bye!' The phone went dead.

Lola stared at her mobile. Samir had been very complimentary about Safi, hadn't he? He said she was really funny . . . Was she, Lola, funny? He was always telling her how nice she looked, but he'd never said she was funny. Was that what Samir liked in a girl?

Did he fancy Safi? What would happen if he did? Presumably Safi fancied Samir, otherwise she wouldn't have given Sienna such a death stare in the store . . .

'Aargh!' Lola said out loud. This was all just too maddening! What she really needed was a way to make sure Samir wasn't going to dump her. Maybe she should try to be funnier. It couldn't be that hard.

Her eyes drooped. Who would have thought that working all day could be so tiring? Hopefully tomorrow would be better. Best to think positive, like the others said. Only four more days to go.

# Chapter 6

## it's nice to be able to make someone happy

It was raining again. But at least Lola had come prepared today and was wearing a thick sheepskin gilet over two cashmere jumpers. Naiha looked similarly wrapped up and Dan grinned at them both. 'Good to see you're wearing a few more clothes today.'

Lola smiled back. Anything to avoid wearing one of those smelly fleeces again!

'You're helping Maggie with the cats this morning,' Dan told them, glancing at a sheet on the wall that had names down the left-hand side and a complicated chart of coloured boxes. 'Make sure you wear gloves too, because we've got one or two that scratch.'

Lola eyed Chalky, who was sitting serenely on the desk as usual and staring out of the window in an I-don't-care-who-you-are kind of way.

The door creaked open and Harry looked in. 'Sorry, didn't realize . . . um . . .'

*He's got really dark eyelashes*, thought Lola, all of a sudden. *I'd have to put on fifty coats of mascara to get mine to look like that.* She blinked. That was a weird thought!

'Everything all right, Harry?' asked Dan.

'Yeah.' Harry glanced at Lola. 'Hi.'

Lola was so taken aback that he'd spoken to her, she forgot to smile. Harry gave a slight shrug and turned to Dan. 'I'm going to work with Groucho again, if that's OK.'

Dan nodded. 'That's fine.'

'Who's Groucho?' asked Lola, trying to make up lost ground, but the door had closed and Harry had gone. *Bother! Now he'll think* I'm *the unfriendly one!*

'Groucho's a Rottweiler,' Dan answered. 'Been here a couple of months and is a bit wild. Harry's training him. If he can get Groucho under control, then he could be rehomed.'

Lola wondered what 'a bit wild' meant. She gulped. Then she suddenly remembered. 'Oh, Dan,' she asked, 'how's Zippy?'

'Who's Zippy?' asked Naiha.

'The rabbit, from yesterday. The one that kept shivering.'

'Oh.' Naiha looked like she didn't remember. 'Yeah.'

Dan made a face. 'Sorry, Lola, she didn't make it.'

'Wh-what?' Lola stared.

'Vet said it looked like a stroke of some kind. It happens sometimes. Ruth told me you'd spotted it. Well done. Sorry not to give you better news, but she died overnight.'

'Oh. Oh, right.' Lola felt numb as she and Naiha walked to the large building that housed the cats. *It's just a rabbit*, she told herself sternly. *And it wasn't even YOUR rabbit!* But she couldn't help feeling upset. Maybe if she'd spotted the shuddering half an hour earlier, Zippy might have made it?

'Cats,' said Naiha, sounding more positive. 'Better than rabbits, at any rate.'

Lola didn't answer. She was remembering Zippy's little body, shivering in her hands. What if she'd been in pain then? A rabbit couldn't exactly tell you how it felt, could it? What if Zippy had been in agony and unable to tell her? Lola felt her eyes fill with tears.

'Hey, look out!' Naiha reached out an arm to stop Lola walking into a stack of buckets.

'Oh. Oh, sorry.'

'Daydreaming again.' Naiha shook her head. 'If you

daydream around here, Lols, you'll tread in poo like I did yesterday.'

Lola tried to smile. 'Yeah.' *She hasn't even noticed I'm upset*, she thought bitterly.

Maggie was waiting for them, her arms full of writhing fur. 'Morning, girls! I hope you're ready for some hard work, we've got lots to do today.'

'Oh, *goody*,' said Naiha in a voice that was so far from pleased it was practically backing out of the building.

'Everyone needs cleaning out, and we've got to load up a few for vaccinations at the vet's too,' went on Maggie, oblivious to or ignoring Naiha's response. 'And they won't like being put in the baskets, so we'll have to do it at the last minute. Have you two brought gloves?'

Lola shook her head. Naiha held out her hands, encased in pale blue wool.

'They won't do,' Maggie told her. 'They won't last two minutes with this lot. You need something much tougher. Borrow some from the cupboard by the door. If you go get two pairs, Naiha, I'll show Lola where you're going to start.'

As soon as Naiha had turned away, Maggie said in a low voice, 'Is everything all right?'

Lola was startled. 'What do you mean?'

'You look a bit upset. Is anything the matter?'

Maggie looked so sympathetic, and her eyes crinkled so nicely at the corners that Lola found herself telling her all about Zippy. 'I don't really know why I'm sad,' she said. 'It wasn't even my rabbit.'

Maggie nodded. 'But it's not nice when an animal dies, is it? Especially one so small and helpless.' She patted Lola's arm. 'It's a good thing that you feel upset. It shows you're the right sort of person to be working here.'

At that moment, Naiha came back with the gloves, and Maggie immediately changed the subject and started explaining how to clean out the cat cages.

Lola was quiet, Maggie's words replaying in her head. *You're the right sort of person to be working here.* That was a weird thing to say! Lola herself would have said she was exactly the *wrong* sort of person to be working at the sanctuary! But in some strange way, Maggie's words gave her a warm feeling inside, like drinking hot soup.

Cleaning out cats was far worse than cleaning out rabbits. 'At least the rabbit droppings don't smell,' said Naiha, wrinkling her nose. 'What do cats *eat* that makes their poo stink so much?'

'I thought you said you had a cat at home?' asked Maggie.

'We do, but it does its business outside,' said Naiha. 'It's got a litter tray but my mum cleans it out every day.'

Maggie smiled. 'Sounds like you've got it easy, then.'

Oddly enough, Lola found she didn't mind the smell as much as she'd thought. *Maybe I'm just getting used to it*, she wondered to herself. The thought was depressing. *Maybe my nose has had as much as it can take and it's shutting down.* She thought longingly of her Lush bath ballistics, arranged in a ceramic bowl in her bathroom, and made a mental note to have one in her bath that very evening, to reinvigorate her nose.

About halfway through the morning, a couple of people came into the building, looking a bit lost. Maggie went over, and Lola could hear them discussing a possible rehoming. 'We'd really like an older cat,' the woman was saying. 'You know, one that's seen a bit of life and deserves a second chance.'

Maggie smiled. 'We've got lots like that. So, a cat aged about two or over?'

'That sounds about right. Or even a bit older.'

Lola raised her eyebrows in surprise. She'd thought most people would want a kitten, if they had the choice.

'What are they doing here?' asked Naiha in a whisper.

'They want to buy a cat,' Lola replied.

'Why don't they get one from a breeder? Or a pet shop or something?' Naiha looked around, frowning. 'I mean, why would anyone come *here* for their pet?'

'I think it's kind of nice,' said Lola. 'To give a cat a chance of a happy family life. Maggie said some of these cats have been really badly treated in the past.'

'Yeah, it makes them aggressive and scratchy.' Naiha held up her arm for Lola to see two long red scratches. 'See this? I know it's wrong to abuse animals, but you can't exactly put them in therapy. If they're all – you know, *broken* – then they should be put down. What if they hurt someone in the new family?'

Lola felt shocked. 'You'd really put down a healthy animal just because it had been abused by a previous owner?'

Naiha shrugged. 'There are always lots more cats, aren't there? It's not like there's a shortage of them.'

Maggie was nearing them with the couple, and she shot them a look. Both girls hastily turned back to work, Lola shaking her head in disbelief. How could Naiha think like that? It wasn't as if Lola herself was about to offer a home to any of these animals, but how could Naiha suggest *killing* animals that had been badly treated? It wasn't *their* fault, was it?

The couple came to stand by Lola, nodding politely to her. 'Tell me about that one,' the woman said, pointing. Lola glanced at her. She was wearing a smart black coat bordered with fake-fur cuffs and collar, ankle boots and an aubergine beret. She was about forty, Lola supposed. The man with her was wearing a woollen beanie, a shirt and jeans. He shivered every now and then, Lola noticed with satisfaction. Clearly she and Naiha weren't the only ones to dress inappropriately for the sanctuary.

'That's Molly,' said Maggie, reaching in for the tortoiseshell. 'She's been with us nearly a year now. Her previous owners brought her in when they had a new baby.'

'Why?' asked the woman. Her voice sounded strained.

Maggie hesitated. 'They read some article about a baby that died when a cat got into its cot and fell asleep on the baby's face.'

The man let out a snort. 'You're joking.'

'No, I'm not. They were frightened.'

'They were stupid,' said the man shortly.

'Martin . . .' said the woman in a soft voice.

Maggie shrugged. 'Having a new baby in the house

makes a lot of people very nervous, and pets can be the focus of that anxiety. We get several dogs a year brought in because of this reason. It's less common with cats but it still happens.'

The man shook his head. 'People read about one freak incident and suddenly everyone's afraid. Drives me mad.'

The woman was looking fondly at Molly. 'What's she like? Is she a friendly cat?'

'Oh, *yes*.' Maggie was enthusiastic. 'She's got a lovely personality. She's always one of the first to greet me in the morning, and she loves being cuddled. Many cats don't, you know – they like to feel independent. Molly can be a bit quiet but she's very responsible, if that makes sense. She doesn't fight to be first for food, and she's been like a mother to little Bella.' She nodded towards the other cat in Molly's cage, a small black one barely out of kittenhood. 'Bella was found in a bin and brought here because the RSPCA didn't have room for her. Molly took her under her wing, so to speak, and Bella has really blossomed.'

'Oh.' The woman's eyes softened. 'I wouldn't want to take Molly away from Bella.'

Maggie smiled. 'I'm sure she'd bounce back. Young cats are very resilient.'

'I know, but . . .' The woman turned to the man.

He saw the look on her face. 'Oh no. We said we were coming for *one* cat, my love. And you said all along you didn't want a young one.'

'But they're like mother and daughter . . .'

He sighed. Then he turned to Maggie. 'We've just found out we can't have any children,' he said quietly. The woman's eyes filled with tears.

'I'm so very sorry,' Maggie said, her voice full of sympathy.

Lola looked away quickly. Suddenly she felt very uncomfortable. She was eavesdropping on a private conversation, and she felt as though she shouldn't be there. Embarrassed, she dropped her bucket with a loud clang. Face bright red, she picked it up, aware that everyone had turned to look. Naiha was smirking. Hadn't she heard what the man said?

The woman ignored the interruption. Her eyes were wet but her face had set in determination. 'Can we take them both?'

Maggie hesitated. 'Are you sure you want two, though? I thought you had decided on just the one?'

'I want them both,' said the woman, nodding. 'Definitely.'

The man opened his mouth, but she shot him such a look that he closed it again.

Lola was relieved when the couple headed over to

the office with Maggie. It was one thing to be cleaning out cats, but quite another to hear people's most private stories.

When Maggie came back, she looked pleased. 'They're a nice couple,' she said. 'I think Molly and Bella will be very happy with them.'

'Will they take them home today?'

'No, Dan will have to go through the paperwork and then one of us will pop over to their house at some point to make sure it's suitable.'

Naiha was astonished. 'Suitable? What do you mean?'

'Well, cats need access to the outdoors. It'd be no good if they lived in a top-floor flat, for example. Or next door to a fierce dog.'

'And you'd refuse to give them the cats if that was what you found?' Naiha stared.

'Of course,' said Maggie. 'We don't hand them over to just anyone, you know. We have to be sure they're going to be well cared for.'

'Otherwise they'll end up here again,' suggested Lola.

Maggie turned to her. 'That's right – you've got it. Once we've checked them out, those two will be able to take Molly and Bella in about a week or so.'

The next time Lola went to empty her bucket,

Naiha came to stand next to her. 'Don't you think it's all a bit ridiculous?' she whispered.

'What do you mean?'

'Well, surely if someone wants one of these cats, they should be able to take them – I mean, what's all this about, checking out their houses? Don't they *want* them to be rehomed?'

Lola cast a sideways glance at Maggie, who had returned to work with a smile on her face. 'But I can see why you'd want to make sure the animals would be cared for,' she said quietly. 'If you've spent a whole year looking after Molly, like Maggie has, then you want to make sure she's going to be OK, don't you?'

Naiha rolled her eyes. 'You're loopy, Lola Cassidy. I think they should be grateful anyone wants to take these cats at all!'

'Sssh.' Lola glanced around. A young guy had just come into the barn, accompanied by an older man.

'Graham!' Maggie called. 'How lovely to see you!'

The young man's face lit up, though Lola was puzzled that he didn't look over to Maggie. Then she noticed that the older man had his hand firmly under Graham's elbow.

'Do you want to have Rocky again?' Maggie asked as

the older man steered Graham to his right. 'I thought, since you got on so well with him last week . . .'

Graham nodded, though his eyes were still fixed on the floor. 'Yes please,' he said, and his voice was slightly thick, as though he had a cold.

Maggie nodded and reached out to take his other arm. 'Come and sit here.'

*He's blind*, Lola suddenly realized. *Graham is blind – what's he doing here?* She watched surreptitiously as Maggie picked up Rocky, a large black and white cat, and placed him on Graham's lap. Graham started stroking Rocky, his face a picture of bliss.

Maggie headed over. 'Haven't you finished yet? You in dreamland today, Lola?'

'No, I – is he, um . . . blind?'

'Yes.' Maggie said it very matter-of-factly. 'He's been blind since birth. Not to mention other problems. But he adores animals.'

'Is he planning to buy one?'

Maggie laughed. 'No, he just comes here to stroke them. He loves it. Been coming here for several months now, just to stroke the cats. Sometimes he strokes the rabbits, but he likes the cats best.'

Lola was puzzled. 'Is that OK? I mean, it's a bit of a weird thing to do.'

'Is it?' Maggie shrugged. 'I don't see it like that.

Graham loves animals but he can't have one himself – he lives in sheltered accommodation. So he comes here once a week to be with them.' She caught Lola's expression. 'Haven't you heard of animal therapy? It's very good for people with disabilities to be around animals – the elderly too. It makes them happy and sometimes it helps them to communicate better.'

'And you don't mind?'

'No, not at all. Besides . . .' Maggie looked over to Graham. His carer gave her the thumbs-up. 'It's nice to be able to make someone happy, isn't it? And it's such a simple thing.'

Naiha was looking at Graham very suspiciously. Lola felt a bit embarrassed. True, Graham was a bit odd-looking, and the fact that his eyes didn't seem to look in the same direction was a bit disconcerting, but his happy expression was strangely moving. To make someone *that* happy just by letting them stroke a cat . . . it *was* kind of nice, wasn't it? She said on impulse, 'Does he want to groom them too? That cat Blubelle has really long fur – we could give Graham a brush . . .' She stopped, aware that Naiha was staring at her.

Maggie smiled. 'That's a great idea, Lola. Blubelle does need a lot of grooming, you're right, and she's one of the few cats who doesn't mind being brushed. Why don't you fetch her from her cage and I'll get the brushes?'

Graham's face lit up even further when Maggie explained what she wanted him to do. Immediately nodding, he began gently combing Blubelle's fur. The cat stretched and purred. Lola felt pleased she'd suggested it.

♥

When the two girls came back from lunch, Dan was in his office, looking concerned. Lola put her bag on the shelf. 'Is everything OK?'

'Yeah.' Dan rubbed his hand through his hair. 'Just another cage falling apart.' He grinned ruefully. 'That's what happens when you put repair on repair. So many of them are too old for proper use.'

'Can't you just buy new cages?' asked Naiha.

'With what?' Dan asked simply.

Naiha shrugged.

'It's all right,' Dan said. 'We've got some repair work planned this afternoon. Though another pair of hands would be appreciated.' He looked hopefully at them.

'Oh,' said Naiha quickly, 'I'm no good at that kind of thing.'

*Neither am I!* thought Lola to herself. *I wouldn't know one end of a screwdriver from another!* 'Er . . .'

Dan smiled at her. 'Don't worry, Lola. It's mostly holding the ladder and keeping track of the screws.'

'OK,' said Lola nervously. She wished she'd answered more quickly than Naiha. What help could she possibly be?

'Thanks. Harry'll be grateful.'

Lola felt her heart sink. 'Oh, I'll be helping Harry?' she asked, wishing even more she'd offered a believable excuse. An afternoon with the silent Harry didn't sound any better than cleaning out the cats. 'I don't think I'm the best person . . .'

'He'll tell you what to do.' Dan clicked on his laptop. 'He's at the back of the rabbit barn. There's a yard there – just walk all the way round.'

The two girls shut the office door behind them. Naiha giggled. 'Good luck.'

'Swap,' begged Lola. 'Please. I just don't know what to say to him.'

'Are you kidding? I'd rather clear up cat poo.'

'He's just so . . .'

'Yeah, totally.' Naiha patted her on the back. 'Never mind, maybe you can give him some grooming tips, eh?' Then she burst out laughing. 'See you later, Lols! Have fun!'

♥

Lola pulled at her hair nervously as she rounded the rabbit barn. The yard was a small area sheltered from the wind, with a makeshift roof of corrugated plastic. It was obviously the place where everything got dumped, from empty sacking to rolls of chicken wire. She felt even less enthusiastic.

Harry was bending over a rabbit hutch door. There was the usual smudge of dirt just in front of his left ear and his boots were caked in mud. *Like some farming shoot*, she found herself thinking, *where they put all the models in denim and cords and make them look as though they work in the fields . . . only Harry's the real thing, and it's not glamorous at all.* She hesitated. They'd got off on the wrong foot, hadn't they? It was time to try again. She smiled her brightest smile, the one that made boys at school open doors for her. 'Hi. I've come to help.'

Harry's gaze flicked up, and an expression of distaste crossed his face. 'Oh, great,' he muttered.

Lola's smile vanished. 'Sorry, am I not what you were hoping for?'

'Not really.' He reached for a hammer. 'Never mind. Pass me those staples.'

Lola said lightly, 'What's the magic word?'

Harry swore. 'I'll get them myself.' He got up, glowering, and fetched a handful of tiny metal pieces from a toolbox sitting open on the other side of the yard. Then he stretched the wire over the wooden frame and carefully tapped in staple after staple to hold it in place. Lola watched, feeling like a spare part. When he'd finished, he sat back and looked up at her. 'You can go back, if you like. I can manage on my own.'

Lola felt stung. 'Dan sent me to help.'

'Then are you going to, or what?'

'I *will* if you'll let me!' *What can I say?* she wondered. *Everything seems to come out wrong!* 'Look, I don't know much about . . . all this stuff. But Dan sent me, so if you need a hand, then I guess I'm it.'

Harry let out a short laugh. But all he said was, 'Do you know the difference between a flat-head and a cross-head screwdriver?'

'Probably,' said Lola cautiously.

'I need a cross-head screwdriver from the toolbox over there,' Harry pointed, 'and six half-inch cross-head screws. Can you do that?'

Lola peered into the toolbox. It was a jumble of plastic packets of nails, screws and things she didn't recognize. Half-inch cross-head screws? What on earth were they? She opened her mouth to say, 'Sorry, I don't have a clue,' but something stopped her. She wasn't stupid, and she hated the idea that Harry might think she was. Surely she could work this out? She started picking through the bags. Some of them were labelled, which helped. She soon knew what cross-head screws looked like. How big was half an inch? Why on earth didn't screws come in centimetres like everything else?

A minute or so later, she held out a handful of items to Harry. 'Are these the right things?'

Harry looked up, a frown on his face. Then his expression relaxed, and he looked surprised. 'Yeah, they are. Thanks.'

Lola felt pleased with herself. 'What do you need next?'

'Can you hold this in place while I screw them in?' Harry held out part of a hinge. 'These doors are always falling off because the wood's gone rotten. I've put a new piece of wood in, and now I've got to put the hinge back on.' It was the longest sentence Lola had heard him say.

'OK. Show me where to hold it . . .'

In the end, Lola had to sit on the concrete in order to hold the door exactly where Harry wanted it. The chill seeped through her jeans and the ground was dirty, but she didn't want to say anything. After all, Harry must be cold too, mustn't he? But he wasn't complaining. *I don't want to give him any more opportunities to look down on me*, she found herself thinking. People didn't usually look down on her – in fact, she was more used to admiring glances and friendly chats. It was a new experience to meet someone who didn't think there was anything particularly special about her, and it made her feel uncomfortable, as though she had to prove herself.

Hoping to encourage him to say more, she asked, 'So, how long have you been working here?'

'A while. Move that to the right a bit. That's better.' He picked up the drill. 'I've got to make some holes for the screws first. Keep it still.'

'This place isn't quite what I expected,' Lola said invitingly.

'Mmm.'

She sighed. Boys liked to talk about themselves, didn't they? At least, the ones she knew did. Maybe that would be a good topic of conversation? 'Have you got any brothers or sisters?'

Harry looked up, distracted for a moment. 'What? Why?'

'I was just wondering.' He was so defensive! What

was wrong with asking about his family? Perhaps she should tell him a bit about herself first. 'I've got two sisters, one younger, one older. The older one's a model in London.'

Harry said nothing, bent back over the door hinge.

Lola searched for something else to say. 'My mum used to be a model too. She was really successful. She married my dad, who was a photographer, and had me and my sisters. And then they split up and now she's married to my stepdad.' She was aware she was starting to waffle. 'You know the Kellerman Health Club?'

Harry grunted.

'He owns it. And the whole chain, actually.'

'Keep the hinge still, otherwise I might drill your hand by mistake.'

Lola gulped and concentrated. She was so close to Harry she could feel his breath on her wrist. He held the drill steadily and confidently. Lola wondered how old he was. He seemed somehow very mature. 'You're really good at this,' she said quietly, almost without thinking.

'Lots of practice,' he murmured, placing a screw precisely in the tiny hole and tightening it with a flick of the wrist.

A few moments later and it was finished. 'Thanks,' he said.

Lola felt pleased. 'You're welcome. What's next?'

He sat back on his heels and looked at her. 'Do you really want to help, or have you just been sent? Because I can get it done without you, you know.'

Lola's pleasure evaporated. 'I thought you needed an extra pair of hands.'

He glanced down at them. 'Those hands don't look as though they've done this kind of thing before.'

'Well, of course they haven't! You don't imagine I sit around all weekend mending stuff, do you?'

A smirk appeared at the corner of his mouth. 'Doesn't seem likely, no. I'm guessing you sit around all weekend having your nails and hair done.'

Lola was insulted, even though it sounded like a nice way to spend a weekend. 'That just shows what *you* know. And there's nothing wrong with wanting to look nice. Not that *you'd* understand that.' Once the words were out, she regretted them. She hadn't meant to be quite that rude!

A genuine grin burst across Harry's face. Lola was taken aback – his eyes sparked into life. It was as though a switch had been flicked – and a dynamic, interesting person was suddenly there. 'You'd be dead right there.'

'Well . . .' she said, suddenly scrabbling for the right words. 'Well, then.'

'Well what?'

'Well, you can't judge someone before you know them,' she said, still rather stunned by the transformation. Her own words reached her ears and she swallowed. *What are you talking about, Lola?*

He nodded thoughtfully, still amused. 'True.'

'So do you want my help or not? I may not have the right sort of hands, but . . . but at least I know what a cross-head . . . um . . . half-inch screw looks like.'

He let out a laugh, and Lola felt her own mouth twitch into a smile, it was such an infectious sound. 'All right, you got me. I've got to patch the roof over one of the dog pens. You up for it?'

'Definitely.'

'Let's get going, then.'

# Chapter 7

## what a pointless way of making money

Lola wasn't quite sure how she felt about holding the bottom of a ladder, Harry's feet just centimetres from her nose. Once or twice, he shuffled on a rung and nearly kicked her in the face. 'Hey!'

'What?'

'Watch it! You nearly kicked me in the nose!'

'What's your nose doing so close to my feet?'

'Holding the ladder still, you moron.'

'You're holding the ladder with your nose?' Harry sounded amused.

'No, I mean . . . Oh, never mind. Haven't you finished yet?'

'Why, are you bored?'

'*Yes.*'

'Tough.' He laughed again.

Lola was taken aback by his concentration

and dedication to the job. They worked for three solid hours and Harry didn't suggest taking a break once. She was determined not to let him outdo her, so she didn't suggest it either, apart from a trip to the toilet because she was desperate. They mended the roof, two more hutches, fixed a fence and made a new shelf for the store cupboard where the food was kept. Harry was incredibly skilled when it came to fashioning repairs out of what looked like rubbish. Dan grinned when he saw the two of them working together. 'A proper little team,' he commented.

Lola flushed, but she felt pleased. She was quite enjoying the work; it was satisfying to see something fixed. She knew that she wouldn't have a clue how to do any of it without Harry, but slowly she was learning the way things were done. When Harry handed her the drill and asked her to make a deep hole in the wall for the wall plug, she was nervous. 'Oh, you do it. I'll make a mess.'

'Don't be stupid. You've been watching me do it all afternoon, it's time you had a go.'

The drill was unexpectedly heavy and Lola nearly dropped it. How was Harry able to wield it so easily? He must be very strong under all those fleece layers. The thought made her blush again. What on earth was she doing, thinking of Harry without his clothes on!

'Just here.' Harry pointed to the pencil mark on the wall. 'Nice and steady.'

Lola lined up the drill and hesitantly pressed the trigger. The drill whirred loudly in her ear and the vibration made her jump.

'Try again,' said Harry, not seeming at all concerned.

*If my family could see me now . . .* Lola thought in wonder. *What would Sienna say? Her jaw would practically hit the floor!* She grinned at the image, and then pressed her lips together firmly. She could do this. It couldn't be that hard, could it?

The drill whirred again and Lola pushed it gently against the wall, surprised at how much resistance there was. 'Is that enough?'

'A bit further,' Harry told her. 'Until the drill bit goes in up to *here*.'

A few more seconds, and Lola pulled out the drill. 'There.'

'Perfect.' He grinned at her and she felt a surge of pride. She'd done it all by herself! And she hadn't made a mess of it!

'Now do the one the other side,' Harry said.

Feeling more confident, Lola lined up the drill again.

In seconds the hole was made, and Harry handed her the wall plug to push in. 'You could have a career as a carpenter at this rate,' he said.

Lola laughed. 'No thanks. Besides, I'm going to be a designer. Or a model, like my sister. I haven't decided yet.'

'Oh, right. The one in London.'

'Yep. She has such a glamorous life, she gets to go to all these parties and films and things.'

'That's what you want, is it?'

She laughed. 'Wouldn't you?'

'What – want to go to posh parties? No way.'

'Seriously? Wouldn't you want to drink champagne and have your photo taken and meet celebrities?'

He shrugged. 'I don't like champagne.'

Lola couldn't think what to say next. 'You'd want to be rich, though. Right? I mean, everyone wants to be rich.'

'Well, yeah, if I win the lottery or something. But not by having my photo taken. I can't stand it. And what a pointless way of making money.'

Lola felt her face fall. There was a cold feeling in her stomach. 'What do you mean, pointless?'

'Standing around all day dressed up so someone can take photos of you? It's not exactly a job, is it?' He looked amused.

'Of course it's a job! There's more to it than just standing there and ...' Lola's voice trailed away. How could she explain? 'It's a skill, just like – like putting up shelves is a skill. You have to learn how to walk, and how to hold your head and ... tons of stuff.'

'How to *walk*?' Harry was chuckling out loud now. 'See, there you go. That's just stupid.' He held the shelf up against the wall. 'You hold this end while I finish this bit.'

Lola felt like screaming in frustration. How could Harry be so dismissive? He knew nothing about it! Modelling was such a demanding job. Helena had told them tales of catching flu from doing winter shoots, hurting her back by standing in five-inch heels, the constant battle to look serene and beautiful when you were so exhausted you could fall asleep standing up. And Quinn's life wasn't all parties either, Lola knew. But the rewards were worth it, weren't they? The money could be amazing and you got to travel the world.

*Well*, thought Lola to herself, *I won't be telling him anything about myself in the future, that's for sure!*

♥

Coming home that evening was such a relief to Lola. The moment she got into Corin's heated Audi with its built-in sat nav and squeaky-clean seats, she relaxed. This was where she belonged – amongst luxury and comfort.

'No Naiha today?' asked her stepfather.

'No, her mum's picking her up.' She turned to wave out of the back window to her friend. Then she said impulsively, 'You'll never guess what I did today.'

'Go on.'

'I put up a shelf. With a drill, and screws and everything.'

Corin glanced sideways at her in astonishment. 'You did what?'

'I know. Can you imagine me with a drill?'

He laughed. 'Did you make a hash of it?'

'*Actually*, I did it just fine.'

He raised his eyebrows. 'Good for you. So you'll be wanting dungarees and steel toecaps for your next birthday, then.'

Lola shuddered. 'Ew. No thanks.'

'Speaking of fashion, the Parchester club is going to have a makeover. We need some shiny new floor-to-ceiling banners to promote the new Pilates and yoga programme, not to mention new furnishings and colour.' He grinned. 'It's going to cost me a fortune but it'll be worth it.'

Lola's heart skipped a beat. 'Can I – can I come and help?' That was exactly the sort of thing she loved doing – matching colours and fabrics and themes!

Corin smiled. 'Sorry, Lola, this one's strictly business. Claire's hired a professional interior design firm.'

'Oh. Maybe I could just come and tell you what I'd do if it were me?'

'I'm sure you'd have some lovely ideas, sweetheart, but this isn't a job for amateurs.' He gave her an apologetic sideways glance. 'Sorry, Lola. Maybe you can come and give your opinion after they've finished.'

'Mmm.' Lola stared out of the window, trying not to show how disappointed she was. She didn't expect her stepfather to put her in charge of the design – of course not – but it would have been nice to be involved. She already knew what colour scheme she'd use for the reception area, which was currently decked out in red and beige.

'Maybe you could be one of the models on the new banners,' Corin suggested brightly. 'In a yoga pose or something. I'll see what Claire says.'

Lola gave a weak smile. 'Thanks.' Normally, she'd have jumped at the chance to do a photoshoot, but she'd rather have been involved in the new design. How could she get Corin to change his mind? She pondered this problem for the rest of the way home, her disagreement with Harry completely forgotten. A bright pink Mini Cooper was parked under the sitting-room bay window. 'Quinn's here!'

'Yes, she got back this afternoon – your mum emailed me.' Corin carefully eased his Audi into the space next to the Mini. 'Quinn wants my special duck recipe for dinner.'

'Ooh, yum. Got to wash first, though. I'm filthy.'

♥

Ten minutes later, after a very quick shower, Lola pulled on her fluffy slippers and padded towards the sitting room, where she guessed Quinn would be. Sure enough, Quinn, Sienna and their mother were comfortably draped over the squashy sofas, a jug of strawberry sunshine mocktail on the glass coffee table between them.

Quinn looked up as Lola came into the room and smiled. 'Hey, gorgeous! I thought I heard you come in a few minutes ago. How's things with you?'

Lola gave her sister a hug, breathing in her Jo Malone perfume and wondering what she had done to make her hair shine so much. 'I'm fine. Sorry, had to wash the cat smell off. You look amazing!'

'So do you.' Quinn took a step backwards. 'You've grown again.'

'Don't be silly, it's only been a couple of months since you saw me.'

'Well, then I forgot how pretty you are,' Quinn said, smiling. She smoothed Lola's hair back from her face. Anyone looking at them would have known instantly they were sisters – in fact, between Quinn, Lola and Sienna the only difference was age and maturity. The same straight blonde hair, blue eyes and slim figures – all three of them took after their mother.

'How's the work experience?' asked Quinn.

Lola pulled a face. 'Don't ask.'

'I'm so sorry it didn't work out at Mulberry. I was really looking forward to having you stay with me.'

'Me too.'

'Come and sit down.' Helena patted the cushion next to her. 'Quinn's been telling us about the Rimmel promotion.'

'It sounds *so* cool,' Sienna said, her eyes shining. 'She's going to be in *Selfridges*, for goodness' sake! On the cards by the make-up stands!'

'Probably,' said Quinn, blushing slightly. 'Though they might end up just using my hands, if I'm not so lucky.' She held them out. The nails were shaped to perfection and painted a bright glossy turquoise. 'I did a hand shoot yesterday.'

'A *hand* shoot?'

'It's really boring, actually,' admitted Quinn. 'It takes ages to get exactly the right picture, and your hands ache and ache.' She smiled ruefully. 'Not as glamorous as the eye shadow shoot!'

'This is her latest portfolio.' Sienna was practically bouncing up and down. She held out the heavy black folder to Lola. 'Go on, it's got the Zara shoot in it and everything.'

Lola opened the glossy book. 'Wow, Quinn!' There were pictures of her sister sitting on a swing as the sunlight filtered through her hair; waist-deep in a field of cornflowers, a ruffled sundress falling off one shoulder; looking straight into the camera, eyes rimmed with liner and pupils wide, reflecting tiny light specks; in an underwear set, the pink bra bordered by lace; reaching out to pat a horse, dressed for a riding lesson ... Lola turned the pages in awe and envy. What an amazing life her sister led! She stopped at a picture of her sister in a long silver evening dress, her face turned toward the camera. Lola's brow creased slightly. 'This one doesn't look like you.'

'They airbrushed it,' Quinn told her. 'They airbrush them all.'

'Well, yeah, when you get a spot on your nose or something . . .'

'No – all of them. They make my eyes bigger, my nose smaller.' Quinn shrugged. 'It's just what they do.'

'But why would they need to make your eyes bigger?' Lola stared. 'Your eyes are fine as they are.'

'But not perfect,' remarked Quinn wryly. 'You can always improve. Haven't you noticed how none of the pictures are really exactly how I look?'

Lola flicked back through the book. Now that she looked more closely, she could see that Quinn was right. In several pictures, her arms looked thinner than they did in real life, and in the lingerie shot, her thighs looked slimmer too. 'You look so skinny in this one.'

'That's all airbrushing too!'

'Let me see.' Sienna came to perch next to Lola on the sofa. 'That's brilliant. Your legs go on for ever! I wish I looked like that.'

'So do I,' agreed Quinn, but there was a funny look in her eyes.

'I think you look gorgeous as you are,' Lola reassured her, though she felt puzzled. Was Quinn unhappy with the way she looked? Why? She was stunning!

'Have a mocktail,' Sienna told Lola. 'I made it.'

The four of them chatted and laughed until Corin called them in to dinner, but Lola was conscious of a slight strain. At first she was confused – was someone unhappy that Quinn had come home? There was something wrong in the atmosphere; it wasn't the carefree fun they'd had at Christmas.

*No*, she realized as they got up from the sofas, *there's something wrong with Quinn herself*. Glancing around, she wondered if anyone else had noticed, but she didn't think so. *What is it exactly?* Quinn wasn't miserable; she answered all their questions with a light laugh and a ready response. Her eyes were bright, her smile wide – she looked happy. Was she perhaps *over*-happy? *Is she putting it on?* Lola wondered suddenly with a shock. *Is the laughter an act?*

No, it couldn't be that. Why would Quinn be unhappy? Modelling was hard work, she knew that, but surely it was worth it for the glamorous lifestyle? On an impulse, Lola asked over dinner: 'Quinn, what's it like being a model?'

Sienna laughed. 'What a silly question! You know what it's like!'

'I've told you often enough,' added her mother, smiling.

'Yes, but Mum' – Lola turned to her – 'things change, don't they? I mean, it's not the same as it was when you were a model. All that airbrushing, for one thing.'

'That's true,' said Helena ruefully. 'Maybe I could have gone on for longer if they'd had airbrushing back then. Instead of being chucked out the minute I developed any lines round my eyes.'

Corin patted her arm affectionately. 'You don't look a day over thirty-five, my love.'

'That's because of the Botox,' said Sienna mischievously.

'Sienna!'

'Well, it's true.'

'Botox is a wonderful invention.' Helena touched her face. 'I don't know what I'd do without it. Ageing is so cruel.' She sighed dramatically.

'Anyway,' said Lola, determined to get the conversation back on track, 'I was wondering what modelling is like for Quinn. I mean, what a typical day is like.'

'There's no such thing as a typical day,' Quinn said, spearing a piece of duck with her fork. 'Every day is different.' Her mouth pushed itself into a smile. 'That's why it's such a cool job.'

'All right,' said Lola, 'tell me about one of your days. What did you do yesterday?'

'The hand shoot for Rimmel, like I told you. Kind of boring.'

'Yes, but . . .' Lola felt frustrated. 'What about the other stuff? I mean, what time do you get up, how long does it take you to get ready, how far do you have to travel, what do you have for breakfast? Those kinds of things.'

Quinn stared at her. There was something in her blue eyes that looked – what? Anxious? Frightened? 'Why would you want to know all that?'

Lola shrugged, sensing she was losing this battle. 'It's part of being a model, isn't it?' she tried. 'Part of that life.'

Sienna was losing interest. 'Oh, who cares about any of that? It's the *parties* I want to know about. And the actors, and the clubs. And the clothes – you are *so* lucky to be given clothes for free!'

Quinn laughed. 'Not always clothes I'd have chosen, Sienna!'

'But the parties,' pursued Sienna.

Quinn hesitated. *Was there a frown there, or did I imagine it?* wondered Lola. But Quinn was smiling warmly now. 'The parties are pretty fab,' she agreed. 'In fact, you'll never guess who I met the other week . . . '

♥

Later that evening, Lola was in bed, reading her copy of *Glamour* magazine and wondering if she could persuade her mother to let her have an Elie Saab dress for the perfume launch. Probably not, though it would be best to wait and see what Helena bought Sienna on their shopping day out tomorrow before she demanded a dress of equal expense. Quinn was going with them, which had surprised their mother. 'Don't you have to get back to London?'

Quinn shook her head. 'I've taken a few days off. There's nothing until Saturday.'

'What happens if something comes in at the last minute?' asked Helena, her voice worried, though her brow stayed perfectly smooth. 'You need to be on the spot for these things; you don't want to miss out. The job will go to someone else.'

Quinn shrugged. 'Then it goes to someone else.' She smiled. 'I can take time off, can't I?'

Lola knew her mother had been puzzled by this, and she had to admit that she was puzzled too – it wasn't like Quinn to deliberately be away from

London. Sometimes the agency could ring in the morning with a job for the afternoon of the same day. With so many girls in the business, you couldn't afford to throw away opportunities. Quinn wasn't yet top of the heap – she didn't have fashion designers or big corporations knocking on her door; she still had to do the rounds of auditions and test shoots. So why would she willingly take time off unless she was ill?

Lola glanced at her clock. It was late and she had work tomorrow, though the sanctuary felt like another world at the moment. *Orange juice*, she decided. *Or milk. Yes, milk – milk will help me stop going over and over things in my head.* She slipped into her fluffy mules and padded silently downstairs.

On her way back up with the milk, a slight noise caught her ear. She paused on the stairs. Helena was on the computer in her study at the end of the landing, but it wasn't the tap-tap of a keyboard that had struck her as odd. She listened carefully.

There it was again! A sort of muffled noise, like a hiccup. Lola put her milk down on the mahogany cabinet at the top of the stairs. Which room? The left? But that meant . . .

The noise came again and Lola, tiptoeing closer, finally realized what it was.

It was coming from Quinn's room. Quinn was

crying, desperately and as softly as possible. *I knew something was wrong!* All of a sudden, she felt guilty for not going to see her sister earlier and asking her if she was OK. Quietly, she knocked on the door.

'Who is it?' came a sharp voice.

'It's me.' Lola turned the handle, but the door was locked on the inside. 'Are you all right?'

'Yes, why shouldn't I be?'

'I thought – I thought I heard you crying.'

There was a slight pause. 'No,' came Quinn's voice, sounding more normal. 'No, that wasn't me. See you in the morning, Lols.'

'But . . .'

'Night!'

Lola sighed. 'Night, Quinn.' She picked up her milk and headed back to her room, thinking.

What could possibly make her beautiful sister with her perfect life and dream job unhappy?

# Chapter 8

## these are Miss Sixty, you know!

'You're with the dogs today,' Dan told them. 'Ian's in charge there but if you don't see him, Harry will show you what to do. You'll need to take the dogs out for their daily walk – he'll go with you the first time.'

Lola twisted her fingers together. Although Harry had been surprisingly good company the day before, they hadn't exactly parted the best of friends. And she wasn't at all keen to work with dogs.

There was a knock at the door. 'Come in!' called Dan.

The door opened, and a stylishly dressed woman with a friendly expression looked in. 'Oh, sorry, I didn't realize you were in the middle of something.'

'It's fine. Mrs Dunn, isn't it? You've come to pick up Sheba.'

'That's right.' A pretty dark-haired girl appeared next to the woman. 'Is she ready?'

Dan smiled. 'Raring to go. I'll just need your mum to sign some paperwork. Do you want to go and pick up Sheba yourself, Tania?'

Her expression brightened. 'Can I?'

'Of course. Lola and Naiha will take you across.' Dan turned to them. 'Sheba is the border collie. Far left – Ian or Harry will show you. In fact, get Harry to open the pen for you since he knows Sheba.'

Lola nodded. She and Naiha led Tania round the side of the office and towards the dog pens. 'Tania?' asked Naiha, her brow furrowed. 'Did you say your name was Tania Dunn?'

'Yes, that's right.' The dark-haired girl looked curious. 'Why?'

'Are you an ice skater? Sorry, I know that's a bit of a random question.'

Lola's eyebrows rose. Of course! They'd been to the Winter Ice Spectacular just before Christmas. Tania had done an amazing routine with her partner.

Tania went pink. 'Yes, that's me.'

'We saw you skate,' Lola told her. 'At Christmas.'

'You were *amazing*!' added Naiha.

'Thanks.' Tania looked pleased. 'It went better than we thought it would.'

'I'd never have dared do all that stuff,' Naiha went on. 'Didn't he lift you over his head at one point?'

Tania grinned. 'Yes. I was a bit terrified by that one.'

'You didn't look it,' Lola said. She'd been spellbound by Tania's routine and now she looked at her with respect. This girl was incredible – look what she could do!

'Well, I have a good partner. I knew he wouldn't let me fall.'

Naiha glanced around before saying, 'Are you and him – I mean . . .'

Tania coughed. 'Uh, yeah. Yeah, we are.'

'He is *hot*,' Naiha said, nodding for emphasis.

Tania gave a laugh. 'You sound just like my friend Libby.'

'Well, he is!'

'Thanks – I think so too.' Tania went even pinker.

Lola was rather sorry they'd arrived at the dog pens; she was keen to know more about Tania and her skating. The local paper was always mentioning the competitions and exhibitions Tania was taking part in. A sudden thought struck her, and she reached out to stop Tania going in. 'I don't suppose you ever go to the Kellerman Health Club, do you?'

'Um, no. Why?'

'My stepfather runs it,' Lola said, wondering if

Corin would mind what she was about to say. 'They're doing a massive makeover soon and they're going to do floor-to-ceiling posters. They need people to be photographed doing gym stuff.'

'Yes?'

'I wondered – do you think you'd be up for doing a shoot? I mean, you can't skate there, but you do ballet and other stuff, don't you? And you're a – a kind of local celebrity.' *It would be a massive scoop for the club! And maybe Corin would let me tell him about my ideas for the redesign if he was pleased with me!*

Tania looked interested. 'I don't know. I mean, yeah, it sounds kind of fun. Hang on . . .' She reached into her bag. 'Let me give you my number. You can pass it on if you like.' She scribbled on a piece of scrap paper. 'There you go.'

'Thanks!' Lola felt excited. She might just have come up with the best idea ever! Harry appeared in a further part of the yard and she called over to him. 'Hi, Harry! Tania's come to pick up Sheba.'

Harry looked up and Lola was conscious of a feeling of surprise. Had he *brushed his hair*? There was something a bit different about it – was that *gel* in it?

'OK,' he said. 'I'll get her.'

'So you and your partner . . .' Naiha wanted to know more.

'Zac,' said Tania.

'Zac, right. Were you and him going out before you started skating together?'

Tania laughed. 'No way. I thought he was a nightmare.'

'Really?'

'But then we started skating as a couple and . . .' She shrugged, smiling. 'You know. Stuff happened.'

Naiha sighed. 'Everyone's fixed up except me.'

'What do you mean?' Tania asked.

'You've got Zac. And Lola's got a boyfriend too.'

Lola felt herself redden and she looked across at Harry, who was leaning over a low pen on the other side of the yard. *Why should I be embarrassed if he hears?* she thought, surprised at her own reaction. *What's it got to do with him?*

'And who have I got?' Naiha thrust out an arm dramatically. A dog shot out of the open pen and leaped up at her, wagging its tail furiously and barking. 'Argh! Get off!'

'Sheba!' cried Tania. The dog immediately turned to her, barking with delight. Tania bent down to stroke her, grinning. 'Hello, darling, we've come to take you home with us.'

Sheba barked again, her tail wagging so hard her back half waved from side to side. 'I think she's pleased to see you,' Lola commented, trying not to laugh at Naiha, who was picking fur off her jacket with a horrified expression.

'I couldn't believe my dad finally said yes to a dog,' confessed Tania, rubbing Sheba under her chin. 'I go away, you see, to skating competitions, and I train so much at the rink I don't know how often I'll get to walk her. But I've always wanted a dog. And Dad says he'll walk her when I can't. She's a sort of late Christmas present.'

'You could hire a dog walker,' suggested Lola.

Tania looked surprised. 'Can you do that? Really?'

'Totally. People do it all the time in London when they're too busy to walk their dogs, I've seen them.'

Tania shook her head. 'Wow. No, I don't think we'd do that.' She grinned. 'My dad would say it's a waste of money, paying someone to do something you can do yourself.' She stood up. 'Come on, Sheba, let's go and find Mum. Thanks for bringing me over here.'

'No problem,' said Lola.

As Tania and Sheba disappeared round the corner, Harry headed over. 'You two in with the dogs today?'

'Yeah,' said Naiha in a bored voice, not looking at him.

'Dan said we'd need to walk them,' Lola added, still puzzling over his hair. It looked *almost* nice.

Harry wasted no time on pleasantries but soon had them kitted out with thick gloves. 'So that you don't get friction burns from the leads,' he explained. 'You take these three,' he said to Naiha, indicating the pen on her left, 'and Lola, you take these four.'

'Three?' said Naiha in horror. 'I can't manage three dogs at once! Are you mad?'

Harry faced her. 'If you're going to walk them one at a time,' he said calmly, 'you won't have got through them all by the end of next week. We have to walk them in groups, they're used to it.'

Lola stared at the dogs Harry had indicated. Two of them were quite little, but the other two were bigger. She felt a chill of fear. 'Harry,' she said quietly. 'Um . . . look. I'm a bit nervous of dogs.'

He turned to look at her, one eyebrow raised.

'I don't want to be difficult,' she added hastily, 'I really don't. But I've never had a dog. And I've always been – uh – a bit scared of the barking.' She reddened, expecting him to scoff at her reluctance.

To her surprise, he nodded. 'All right. Let me show

you.' Reaching in to the first dog, he spoke to it in a calm but firm voice. 'Daisy, we're going for a walk now and I need you to be a good girl. That's it. Stand still.'

To Lola's surprise the dog, who had been jumping up and down in excitement, trotted out and stood patiently as Harry clipped on her lead. Lola could see Daisy trembling with eagerness, but she didn't move from the spot while Harry got the other three dogs ready, speaking all the time in a calm but firm tone.

'You see?' Harry turned back to Lola, still keeping the same way of speaking. 'The dogs need to feel secure with you. They look up to you; they'll expect you to tell them what to do. It's a bit like expecting a teacher to take control of a class. If he doesn't, then you know you can get away with anything.'

Lola swallowed, her throat dry. 'I've got a French teacher like that. She's hopeless.'

'There you go – it's the same with dogs. These four are all really friendly, and they never bite. But they do get excited about going for a walk, so the only thing you need to worry about is making sure they don't go too fast.' He looked at her. 'All right?'

'I'll try.'

'Good.' He carefully passed the leads to Lola. She could feel the dogs pulling slightly as she took hold. 'Talk to them,' Harry told her. 'Tell them you're in charge.'

'Er – OK.' She felt very silly. 'Hello, dogs.' They looked up expectantly. 'We're going for a walk today.' She stopped.

'That's good,' Harry said. 'Just make sure you sound a bit firmer. Tell them how you want them to behave.'

'I don't want you to pull on the leads,' Lola said, wondering if the dogs understood anything of what she was saying. Out of the corner of her eye she could see Naiha trying to stifle a giggle. 'And I want everyone to walk nicely while we're out. Otherwise – otherwise we'll come straight back.'

Harry grinned. 'You sound just like my old art teacher.'

'Is that good?'

He gave an amused shrug. 'I never mucked about in her lessons.'

Lola felt pleased. Maybe handling dogs wouldn't be so nerve-wracking after all.

Harry turned to Naiha. 'I'll get your three out now.'

Naiha didn't say anything to her dogs when Harry

handed them over, but Lola could see that her friend gripped the leads tightly. Was Naiha as nervous as she was?

'Try the talking thing,' Lola said quietly.

Naiha glanced at her. 'Are you kidding? I'm not talking to the dogs like some weird animal whisperer. I'll feel stupid.'

Lola shrugged. 'Suit yourself.' Inside, she felt irritated. Why did Naiha have to make things so difficult sometimes?

Naiha was eyeing one of her dogs with mistrust. 'I swear this one's a pit bull,' she muttered. 'If it bites me, I'm going to sue . . .' Her voice trailed away as she saw Harry coming back, a Doberman in each hand. 'Um . . .'

'Ready?' he asked. Then without waiting for an answer, he set off, the dogs pulling powerfully at their leads.

'I think we got off quite lightly,' Lola whispered to Naiha.

Naiha made a strangled sound, and the two of them followed Harry.

It was very difficult trying to keep the leads from getting tangled. The dogs might be well behaved, but they kept wanting to sniff different things, or cross in front of each other. Lola had to keep stopping to avoid tripping over the leads. By the way Naiha was swearing, she guessed her friend was having the same problem. 'Cats don't behave like this,' she heard Naiha mutter at one point.

They took the dogs on a large loop, following the pavement alongside the road and then cutting left, through a snicket into a medium-sized park, where the dogs went wild, sniffing everything they could reach. 'Can't we let them off the leads?' Naiha asked.

Harry shook his head. 'Not here, no. It's a residential area, and we've got too many dogs anyway.' He glanced across at Lola. 'You doing all right?'

She was grateful for his kindness. 'Yes, thanks. It's not as hard as I thought.'

He nodded. 'It's just practice. And not letting yourself panic.'

'It's only because it's all new to me. I was scared by a dog when I was little. I've sort of avoided them since.'

'Happens like that for some people.' He grinned suddenly. 'We'll have you taking out the Rottweiler tomorrow.'

Lola went pale. 'No, please, I don't think . . .' Then she saw his expression. 'Oh, you're joking. Thank God.'

Harry let out a snort of laughter. 'Maybe not this week.'

'Maybe not *ever*,' she retorted, smiling back at him.

One of Naiha's dogs squatted down. 'That is *so* disgusting,' Naiha said, trying to look the other way and getting tangled in a lead.

'You'll need this.' Harry passed her a small plastic bag. 'For the poo.'

She stared at him. 'You are *kidding*.'

He shrugged.

'I'm not picking up its *poo*. This is grass, it'll biodegrade.'

'People walk through here,' Harry told her. 'And besides, it's illegal.'

'Who's going to know?'

'Everyone,' said Harry firmly. 'We exercise the dogs here every day. We don't want to be landed with a fine for thousands of pounds.'

A mutinous look in her eyes, Naiha bent to pick up the dog's mess with the bag. Despite the fact she was wearing thick gloves, she managed to hold the bag by the fingertips only. She nudged the poo with her foot, trying to get it into the bag, and at that moment, two of her dogs decided to run in different directions at the same time. Naiha tripped on the suddenly taut leads, lost her balance and sat down heavily on the ground, narrowly missing the little brown pile. She swore again, letting go of one of the leads by mistake. The brown and white dog dashed off immediately, delighted to be free.

Harry swore too. 'Hold these,' he said to Lola, handing her the leads for his two enormous dogs.

'But I—'

'*Sit*,' he said firmly, and for an absurd moment Lola thought he was talking to her. Her knees buckled of their own accord – just as the two Dobermans sat down on the grass. Heart thumping, she watched Harry run after the escaped dog. She felt frozen to the spot. She was in charge of *six* dogs at once! And two of them were nearly as big as she was! The dogs shuffled and panted and Lola's hands clenched the leads so tightly that she couldn't feel her fingers.

Less than a minute passed before Harry returned with Naiha's dog, talking to it sternly. The dog seemed apologetic. Harry handed the lead back to Naiha. 'Don't let go again,' he told her.

'All right, all right.' Naiha was more concerned about the large damp patch on her jeans. 'These are Miss Sixty, you know! If I can't get these grass stains out . . .'

Harry ignored her. 'Thanks,' he said, taking the leads for his dogs back from Lola. 'You OK?'

Lola breathed out. 'Yeah. Yeah, just about.'

He gave her a funny look but didn't say anything else.

The loop took them through the park and out the other side, bringing them back to the centre from the opposite direction they'd set out. Lola's heart rate had returned to normal, and she checked her slim silver watch – it had taken them thirty-five minutes. 'How many more dogs need exercising?' she asked Harry.

'As many as you can fit in this morning,' he said, somewhat preoccupied with the larger of the Dobermans which was barking loudly at a large black mongrel. 'Quiet, Pistol! You should be able to make at least six more trips before lunch and I can do the rest this afternoon.'

'Six!' Lola was appalled.

'All right, five.'

Lola glanced at Naiha, who hadn't heard. 'We can't do that many,' she pleaded in a low tone.

'Why not?' Harry was untying the dogs one by one and putting them back in their pens. 'Check with me or Ian about which ones you take out together, though. They're used to going out in particular groups. And some of them only I can take out because they're difficult to handle.'

'Aren't you coming with us?' If Harry didn't come with them, Lola wasn't at all sure she'd feel confident about handling the dogs. And what if another one ran off?

He shook his head. 'You know the route now, it's not like you can get lost.'

Lola panicked. 'I don't think I can do it without you.'

He gave her an impatient look, but as his eyes met hers, they seemed to soften slightly. 'You'll be fine,' he said in an unexpectedly kind tone. 'I wouldn't let you go out if I didn't think you could do it.'

'Oh.' Lola felt strangely warm inside.

'Besides,' went on Harry, 'I've got too much to do. Ruth said she saw a rat in the rabbit food shed last night as she was closing up. I've got to go sort it out.'

*Sort out a rat?* Lola didn't even want to think about what that meant. 'Why you?'

'Why not? See you later.'

'But—' It was too late. Harry had gone.

Lola and Naiha managed to get the dogs back into their pens and then Lola broke the bad news.

'We've got to do it again?' Naiha said, baffled. 'But we've just walked the dogs.'

'Harry said all of this lot need doing too.' Lola gestured towards the other pens, triggering a volley of barking as the dogs realized it might be their turn next for a walk. 'He reckoned we could do five or six more trips before lunch.'

'*Five or six?*' Naiha was speechless for a moment. 'This is beyond a joke,' she said eventually. 'This is slave labour. They can't *make* us do it.'

Lola bit her lip. 'No . . . but it's part of our work experience, isn't it? I mean . . . what about our assignments at school?' *I can't believe I'm trying to persuade my best friend to take a bunch of dogs out walking with me. What parallel world have I slipped into?*

'Stuff them,' said Naiha tartly. 'I don't give a monkey's.'

A tall thin man with greying hair and a growing bald patch came round the corner. 'Hi there,' he said cheerfully, 'you must be the work experience girls. Harry says you need to know which dogs to take out.'

'Well—' Naiha started to say, but Ian either didn't hear her or didn't want to let her speak.

'Rosie, Bramble, Sir Lancelot and Scar work well as a group,' he said. 'And Big Bill, Ginny and Demon don't fight each other. Though you'll need Demon on one hand and the other two together. He pulls very strongly.' He eyed up the girls. 'You'd better take that group,' he told Lola, who was pleased he thought she looked strong, but terrified at the thought of a dog called Demon. She wasn't sure she could remember how to speak calmly yet firmly. 'I'll get them out for you and swap them over when you get back, so you don't have to hang around between walks. Don't forget the poop bags.'

Before the girls could utter any kind of protest, Ian had bundled the dogs out of their pens and onto leads and into the girls' hands. Within minutes, Lola and Naiha found themselves being pulled towards the gates by seven overexcited dogs. 'This is a nightmare,' Naiha moaned as she was dragged along.

'Walk *nicely*,' Lola admonished the dogs, but this group was less well-behaved than the last one, and they took no notice. Heart racing, she was forced to half run to keep up with them.

By twelve o'clock the girls were exhausted. 'My hands stink of poo,' wailed Naiha. '*Again.*'

Lola had decided that although dogs weren't as scary as she'd previously thought, they were a lot *stronger*.

'Last lot,' said Ian. His cheerfulness grated on

the girls. 'Then you can stop for lunch and a sit down.'

'Can't we stop *now*?' whined Naiha.

'What?' Ian tilted his head. 'Didn't hear you.'

'I *said*, I can't do any more. I'm knackered.'

'I've got the dogs all ready,' Ian said, looking put out. 'They won't like it if you lock them up again. Go mad, they will.'

Naiha looked apprehensively at the last group, which was bouncing up and down, tongues hanging out. 'My feet hurt.'

'So do mine,' added Lola.

At that moment, Harry came back into the yard, holding a large dead rat by its tail. 'All right?' he said.

The girls stared at him. 'What . . .' said Naiha in a wobbly voice, 'is *that*?'

'What? Oh, this?' Harry held out the rat. 'It's a rat. Obviously.' He looked from one to the other. 'What?'

'You're just holding it by the – the *tail*,' said Lola, aghast.

'Best bit to hold it by,' Harry informed her. 'That way they can't bite you. Of course, this one's dead.' He grinned.

Lola was torn between disgust and awe. He'd

actually caught and killed a rat! That was – that was totally revolting, of course, but somehow also incredibly impressive.

'You just taking out the last group?' Harry asked. He nodded. 'Good work.'

'Well, actually . . .' Naiha began, the familiar whinge back in her voice.

'Yes,' said Lola firmly, 'we *are*.' *If he can kill a rat with his bare hands, then I can definitely take a few dogs for a walk!*

'Cool,' said Harry. 'See you in a bit.'

'Why did you say that?' Naiha hissed as they set off once again towards the gates. 'Are you trying to get off with him or something?'

'*What?*' Lola's jaw dropped, even though she was struggling to keep her dogs under control. 'No *way!*'

'Can't think why, he's got a face like the back of a *horse*.'

'He's not as bad as all that. *Sit*, Drac, *sit!*' Dracula, a black Labrador, sat obediently, tail wagging.

'OMG!' said Naiha, coming to a stop. 'You *do* fancy him!' She stared at Lola in horror.

'I do not! Why would I fancy him when I'm going out with Samir?' Lola asked, feeling her hackles rise. Honestly, she knew Naiha was fed up with all the walking, but why did she have to take it out on Lola?

'You tell me.' Naiha shrugged. 'Maybe you like the rough and dirty look.'

'You're being stupid.' Lola was starting to feel fed up herself. Dracula pulled again at his lead.

'All that helping him with his hammer and nails stuff.' Naiha raised her eyebrows suggestively. 'Spending all that time with him yesterday.'

'If you *must* know, we spent half the time arguing!'

'Proves it,' said Naiha with a wave of her hand. 'Opposites attract. And he couldn't be *more* opposite to us.'

'Naiha, you're imagining everything.'

'Really?' remarked Naiha acidly. 'Then why do you blush whenever Harry turns up?'

Lola stared in astonishment. 'I do *not*!'

'You totally do.' Naiha snorted. 'You are so full of it, Lola Cassidy.' Allowing her dogs to pull ahead, she ran a few paces so that she didn't have to talk to Lola.

Lola followed, stung. She did *not* blush when Harry showed up! If she went a bit pink, it was because she knew he looked down on the two of them, and she didn't like it. It was *definitely* not because she fancied him! *Who would fancy him anyway?* she said to herself.

*He's rude and messy and prefers dogs to people. He's nothing compared to Samir!* Though she had to admit that Samir wouldn't know how to train a violent dog or mend a fence or . . . Oh, for goodness' sake! Why would she *need* him to? 'Harry is not boyfriend material,' she told the dogs firmly. 'And even if he was, I've already *got* a boyfriend.' Custer barked loudly as though he agreed.

She tried to catch up with Naiha, but Dracula had decided to pick that moment to do his business against a lamppost, and Naiha was already rounding the corner to the parkland. 'Dracula, no! Not there – oh, how embarrassing . . .' Closing her eyes, she wished she could be anywhere else but here. She just hoped nobody who knew her would come by and see her walking three dogs, one of which was doing an enormous poo on the pavement. She turned her face away from the road. 'Hurry up, Dracula . . .'

The terraced houses on this part of the road were small and dingy, their front gardens cramped and littered. Lola couldn't imagine living in one of these dirty-looking run-down places. OK, so maybe not everyone had lots of money, but surely they could make sure their houses looked nice, couldn't they? It didn't take much to ensure that rubbish was put in bins and not strewn across the front lawn. The house directly in front of her was the worst of the row. Builders' rubble was piled up in the front garden; paint peeled off the window frames, and the outside of the house had once been white but now looked as though it had been in a mud fight. The downstairs front windowpane was broken in the corner, and a plank of wood hung lopsidedly from the sill. *It looks like it was boarded up at some point.* Lola shook her head. They couldn't even remove the planks properly! *Now, if I lived there*, she thought dreamily, *I'd have it all cleaned up and resprayed white, with red window frames. With a bit of imagination, it could look half-decent . . .*

The side gate to the house suddenly opened and Lola looked away, embarrassed to be caught staring. To her great relief, Dracula had finished his business and was now sniffing the low wall, wagging his tail with excitement.

A man came out of the gate and up the little path towards the road, and Lola bent to the ground with her poop bag to avoid looking at him. A smell of sweat and cigarettes reached her nose. Just too late, she realized that Dracula was right in front of the path. The man swore as he reached them and kicked the dog out of the way. Dracula yelped in protest.

'Hey!' Lola straightened up, about to protest further,

but the man turned to look at her and the courage froze in her throat.

He was unshaven, his hair greasy, and his expression unpleasant. 'He's in my way.' His voice was rough and deep. 'And if you're in my way, you'll get a kick too, you little—'

Lola's eyes opened wide in shock at the name he called her. She'd heard bad language, of course, but no one had ever insulted her like this. Fear swept over her. The man was big, and Naiha had already disappeared round the corner. There was no one to see – what if he hit her?

But to her trembling relief, he had turned on his heel and was crossing the road away from her. Lola put out a hand to the low wall. Her knees were shaky and she felt like she was about to cry. The dogs, sensing something was wrong, whined. Dracula sat down and licked his paw.

'Are you all right, Dracula?' She was afraid he was hurt. She'd have to tell someone when they got back. Why had the two girls argued on *this* walk? Lola would have felt much safer if she hadn't been on her own. Naiha was better at standing up to people, though Lola conceded even she probably wouldn't have confronted that man. *I'd have felt much safer with Harry*, she thought, and then felt embarrassed, even though there was no one to see.

Pulling herself together, Lola checked that she had the leads tightly in her hands and, taking a shaky breath, said, 'Come on, then,' to the dogs. But as she took a step, she heard a faint noise coming from the house. A sort of high howl. Lola's eyes went automatically to the front window. What was that? Was someone hurt in there?

Desperately, she looked around. What should she do? She thought of her mobile phone – should she call someone? The police? But she couldn't say she'd just heard a funny noise and that a man had been rude to her, could she? Hesitating, she heard the howl again. Someone was in pain.

'Right.' Lola made a decision. Tying all three dogs to the broken gatepost, she told them firmly, 'Wait here.' The dogs looked up uncertainly. 'Sit.' They sat. *Wow*, she thought, *it worked!* 'I'm only going to look in the window.'

Glancing nervously down the road, she saw that the man had gone, but there was no telling when he'd be back. Quickly, she made her way to the front window, careful not to trip over the pieces of brick and glass scattered across the ground.

The window was grey and grimy and it was

difficult to see in. There wasn't much furniture, only something that looked like a sofa with a dirty blanket thrown over it. The howl came again, much louder this time, and Lola frowned as she peered in, cupping her hands around her eyes to try to see better.

She had thought the room was empty, but then she saw, huddled by the end of the sofa, a small form on the floor. *That's not a person*, was her immediate thought. Then a little nose lifted to the window and she realized it was a dog. A smallish dog, with fur so matted it was hard to tell what type of breed it was. It looked hopefully up at the window and its ears pricked forward. Then it got slowly to its feet and took a few steps towards her. One leg was lifted off the floor – *It's hurt*, thought Lola in horrified fascination. *Is the leg broken?* She lifted her hand to wave to the dog, but the sudden movement had a drastic effect. The little dog flinched visibly and then scuttled behind the sofa as quickly as its injured leg could allow.

'No!' Lola called through the window, knowing it was futile. 'I'm not going to hurt you!' But the dog did not reappear.

*What should I do?* Lola was taken by a sudden urge to try the front door, but the thought of being caught by the returning man was too scary. He must be the owner of the dog, mustn't he? What would he do to Lola if he caught her breaking into his house?

Terror flooded through her and she rushed back to the three dogs, who were getting impatient. Untying them, she headed straight for the parkland, heart thumping and mind racing. *I must tell Dan*, she thought. *As soon as I get back. He'll ring the RSPCA or something. Someone has to go in and save that dog.*

Automatically, she picked up dog mess in the bags, hardly thinking about the three she was in charge of. Her mind was entirely on the sorry little animal she'd seen through the window. She hurried the dogs along, almost running back to the sanctuary, and caught up with Naiha just as she was turning into the gates.

'There you are!' Words tumbled out of Lola as she tried to explain what she'd seen.

Naiha wrinkled her nose. 'What are you talking about? What dog?'

'Through the window. Oh, Naiha, it's horrible. We have to do something.'

Naiha stared at her. 'What do you mean? Do what?'

'It's hurt.'

'Then its owner will take it to the vet.'

'You didn't see it!'

'Lola, it's nothing to do with you.' Frowning, Naiha

handed her four dogs back to Ian, who beamed benevolently at her, entirely deaf to the conversation. 'I'm going for a sit down, my feet are killing me.'

'Naiha—'

'Oh, for God's sake. Why don't you tell *Harry*, Lola? I bet he'd be interested.' Turning, she headed off toward the office.

Lola had completely forgotten her previous argument with Naiha, but now the words struck her with relief. Of course – Harry! He'd know what to do. 'Have you seen Harry?' she asked Ian.

'What?'

'*Have – you – seen – Harry?*'

He pointed to the far end of the dog pens. 'Over there.' Then he grinned, exposing a gap in his front teeth. 'Young love. You ain't the first and you won't be the last.'

Lola didn't bother to contradict him. 'Look, I'm going to find him. Can you check Dracula? This horrible man kicked him and he yelped.'

Ian frowned in concern. 'Which side?'

'Er – left. No, right. The right side. I think he's OK, but I don't know how to check.'

Ian nodded, all his attention now on Dracula, who was bounding around and showing no signs of distress. 'Leave 'im with me. I'll check him out.'

'Thanks.' Lola handed over the leads and headed across the yard.

Harry was refilling the water bowls one by one. He looked up in surprise as she approached. 'What's the matter?'

Lola took a breath. 'I've seen a dog – not one of ours. It's in a house, down on the main road. I think it needs our help.'

Harry's eyes narrowed. 'Which house?'

She described it. 'And this – this man came out of it.' She faltered, remembering the feeling of fear when he had turned on her. 'I guess it's his dog, so . . .'

Harry nodded slowly. 'I know the house you mean. It's been abandoned for months. He's probably squatting there.'

'You mean – it's not his house?' Lola was taken aback. 'But . . .'

Harry put down the water canister. 'We should go now. Before he comes back.'

She took a step backwards. 'What?'

'Come on.'

'Shouldn't we tell someone? I mean, the RSPCA or – or Dan?'

Harry's face darkened. 'Wasting time. Besides, if he's squatting, who knows how long he'll be there?

He could be gone by this afternoon. They won't get to him as fast as we can.'

'Er . . .' Lola was beginning to wish she hadn't told him. The last thing she wanted was to go back to that house, with the possibility of running into that man again. 'Don't you think it's dangerous?'

He was stuffing something into his pocket. 'Not as dangerous as it is for the dog. Come on.'

'Well . . .'

He turned to look at her, finally registering her reluctance. 'Aren't you coming?'

Panic flashed through her mind. Headlines: SCHOOLGIRL MURDERED BY HOMELESS MAN. MODEL OF THE FUTURE CUT DOWN TOO EARLY. Her breath shook. What about her family? A sudden vision of her mother, weeping, distraught: *She was my prettiest little girl . . .*'

'What about the dog?' Harry asked quietly.

Her breath steadied. She looked up at him, at his steady gaze. 'OK. I'm coming.'

# Chapter 9

## we could go to prison for this!

Harry told Dan briefly that he and Lola were going to lunch. Lola avoided Naiha's gaze as they passed her on their way out. Naiha was busy texting, and Lola wondered if she would text Samir and tell him she thought Lola was two-timing him. For a moment, she hesitated. Should she ring Samir herself before Naiha had a chance? But there wasn't time, and if there was any explaining to do, she'd have to do it later. Samir was sensible; he'd know she wouldn't cheat on him.

They reached the house within five minutes, Lola hurrying to keep up with Harry's long stride. 'In the front room, right?' Harry asked quietly as they stood by the front door.

'Yes.'

'You keep a lookout.'

'Shouldn't we knock first? I mean,' Lola gulped, 'to make sure that man isn't back.'

He hesitated a moment and then nodded. 'Fair enough.' He knocked loudly twice.

There was a soft whimpering from inside, and Lola's heart lurched. That poor little thing! It was probably terrified! But no one came to the door or shouted at them to go away. Harry knocked again, louder this time. Again there was no answer except for the muffled whimpers.

'Right.' He turned the handle on the door but it was locked.

'How are we going to get in?'

'You keep watching the road.' Harry reached into his back pocket and pulled out a couple of unidentifiable objects.

'What are those?'

'Never mind.' He bent down and carefully poked them into the lock. Within a few moments there was a click. He tucked the objects back into his pocket and turned the handle. The door swung open.

Lola was shocked. 'You picked the lock!'

'So?'

'How did you know how to do that?'

Harry looked uncomfortable. 'S'not the first time,' was all he would say.

Lola felt a thrill of fear mixed with anticipation. They were breaking into someone's house! She was actually doing something criminal! 'We could go to prison for this!' she said in an agonized whisper.

'Hurry up and come in before someone sees us, then,' Harry snapped back, and she realized that although he looked confident, he must be nervous too. She stepped in and pushed the door to behind her. There was a scuffle from their right.

'This way. Don't frighten the dog.'

Lola screwed up her nose. 'This place stinks . . .' It was a horrid smell – damp mixed with rotting food, beer and urine. There was torn newspaper all over the floor and it stuck to her boots. She felt sick.

Harry had bent down and was edging into the front room, which was dingy in the grey winter light. 'Here, doggie. I've got something for you.' He pulled out a dog treat and held it out in front of him. 'We're here to help you . . . Aah, there you are . . .'

Lola leaned into the room, trying not to touch the walls. The little mongrel was huddled by the sofa, trying to stay out of sight. *It looks so frightened*, she thought, and she wanted to cry again. If the dog was that frightened of humans, how badly it must have been treated! Lola hadn't ever wanted a dog of her own, but at that moment she felt overwhelmingly that she just wanted to take this one home, look after it and keep it safe.

Harry spoke softly and gently to the dog, never raising his voice above a murmur. Lola watched him in fascination. It was a softer version of his 'calm but firm' voice and it made him seem far more vulnerable and affectionate. *In fact*, she thought in surprise, *he looks much younger suddenly*. Slowly, hesitantly, the dog edged out from behind the sofa, sniffing the air. The treat in Harry's hands was obviously too much for it to bear and Lola wondered when it had last been fed. It was painfully thin and its fur was thick with dirt. It limped towards Harry, its eyes wary, ready to flinch away.

'Don't move,' murmured Harry and Lola blinked as she realized he was talking to her.

'I won't,' she breathed back, her voice even quieter than his. Something deep inside her tingled – it was exciting, waiting for the dog to respond.

It reached Harry's hand and took the treat, swallowing it in one gulp, but Harry didn't move. *Why isn't he just grabbing it?* Lola wondered. *Now, before it runs away again!*

But Harry waited, still talking gently to the dog. Afterwards, when she replayed the scene in her head, Lola tried to remember exactly what he said to the dog but she couldn't; it was simply a soothing murmur, almost hypnotic.

The dog sniffed at his hand again, and Harry very slowly reached for another treat. The dog gulped it down eagerly, and there was a hesitant movement of its tail. 'We're getting there,' whispered Harry. 'Not long now.'

*He's a magician*, thought Lola, unable to tear her gaze away. *It's magic, what he's doing.*

It wasn't long before the dog was allowing Harry to stroke it, and it looked much happier. Harry waited before attempting to pick it up, but when he did, the dog lay placidly in his arms, only yelping when Harry brushed against its injured leg. 'I think it might be broken,' Harry said quietly to Lola.

Tears sprang to her eyes. 'How could anyone do that to a dog?'

'I don't know. I never understand it.'

Her gaze swept the dirty room. 'It's disgusting in here – how could anyone live like this?'

Harry raised his eyebrows. 'He's homeless.'

'That doesn't mean you have to live in filth.' Sympathy for the dog made her angry with the man who owned it.

Harry looked down at the dog in his arms. 'It's not always that easy.'

'Oh, you'd know, would you?'

His eyes flashed – something dangerous in them. 'Yes,' he said. 'I would.'

They stared at each other. Lola was speechless. Had Harry been homeless, then? Was he homeless now? She'd never wondered about where he lived – surely he didn't sleep at the sanctuary at night?

The dog made a snuffling noise and nudged Harry's hand. Harry blinked, as though suddenly remembering where he was. 'We should go,' he said.

Lola turned away as a shadow fell over the room. Alarmed, she looked up at the window. 'He's back! We need to get out!'

'Too late,' said Harry grimly. His arms tightened slightly around the dog.

'Hey!' The big man stood in the doorway, glowering at them. 'What the hell do you think you're doing?'

# Chapter 10

## *if you fancy him, then just say so*

The world spun and Lola reached out to steady herself. How could they have been so stupid as to stand around chatting instead of getting out? And now they'd been caught! And probably the best that could happen would be that the man would make them give the dog back. She shuddered to think what the worst might be. *Nobody knows where we are,* she realized. Naiha knew Lola had been upset about a dog, but everyone assumed she and Harry were on a lunch break together. If – if this man kidnapped them, how would anyone ever find them?

'What are you doing here?' the man asked again. He was even taller than Lola remembered and his eyes blazed with fury. 'Put that dog down.'

Harry stood still. 'No,' he said.

The man took a step into the hallway. 'Put it down or you'll be sorry.'

Lola tugged at Harry's sleeve. 'Harry . . .' *What if he has a knife? What if . . . ?* Her thoughts ran away with her. 'Just give it to him . . .'

'No,' said Harry firmly, though Lola wondered if she imagined a tremor in his voice. 'It's injured. It needs to see a vet.'

The man growled. 'It's none of your business. That's *my* dog.' He reached out towards the animal, which let out a high yelp of terror and tried to burrow into Harry's jacket.

'It's terrified of you,' said Harry. 'It's malnourished and filthy. You obviously don't know how to look after a dog.'

Lola gasped. Had he actually said that? Didn't he know how dangerous the situation was?

The man's jaw dropped. Then his eyebrows drew together and his lip curled nastily. 'You've got a nerve, breaking into my house. You'd better watch it, or you'll get what's coming to you.'

'It's not your house,' said Harry. 'You're squatting. And don't threaten me or I'll call the police.'

'Police?' The man's eyes flicked uneasily to one side.

'Yes, police.' Harry pressed home his advantage.

Lola held her breath.

'Do you know what you get for animal cruelty?'

he went on. 'You can be fined thousands of pounds. You can be sent to prison for up to a year.' Harry took a step forward. 'Lola,' he said over his shoulder, 'get out your phone. Dial nine-nine-nine.'

*I haven't got my phone!* Lola thought desperately. *I left it in my bag in Dan's office!* 'OK,' she said shakily and put her hand into her pocket. It was the only thing she could think of. *Maybe if I turn away and mime putting a phone to my ear, he'll think it's a real one . . .*

'All *right*!' the man snarled. 'Have it your way. Take the mutt; and good riddance!'

Lola staggered with relief. *It worked! He really thought I was going to phone the police!*

Without a word, Harry strode past the man and out of the house. Lola followed him, tripping over the doorstep in her haste and not daring to look at the man as he stood aside and glared at them.

The two of them said nothing until they were nearly back at the sanctuary gates. Lola could hardly believe what had just happened. 'Harry . . .' she gasped, still glancing around fearfully to see if the man was following. 'Harry, slow down . . .'

Harry stopped so suddenly she nearly bumped into him. 'You all right?' he asked gruffly, as though he'd only just noticed her.

'I'm OK, I think. But Harry – back there. You were amazing!'

Harry snorted. 'He's a bully. You just have to stand up to people like that.'

'I wouldn't have *dared*!'

He looked faintly amused. 'You went along with it, though. You and your pretend phone!'

'You *knew* I didn't have my phone with me?'

He shrugged. 'You're not carrying your little bag. I guessed maybe it was back here.'

'And you *still* . . .' Lola took a breath. 'That was a total risk, Harry.'

He frowned. 'It had to be done. I wasn't leaving without the dog.'

They both looked down at the dog in his arms. It was trembling and trying to tuck its nose under Harry's arm.

Lola felt tears rising to her eyes. 'Is it going to be OK?'

'I don't know,' said Harry shortly. 'But she needs proper help right now.'

'It's a girl?' Somehow that made Lola feel even sorrier for the little dog.

'Yup. We have to take her to Dan.'

'But . . . but what are you going to tell him?'

Harry seemed puzzled. 'The truth, of course. What else would I tell him?'

Two minutes later, they were both standing in Dan's office while he carefully looked over the trembling dog. Lola was silent as Harry told his boss exactly what had happened, right from Lola spotting the dog to the confrontation with the man in the dirty house. *I can't believe he's telling him the truth*, Lola thought. *We are going to be in so much trouble! We could have told him anything – we found the dog by the road, or it was hiding in a front garden by itself – anything! And now Harry's telling him how we broke into someone's house!* She stared stonily at the floor, wondering if this was going to get back to the school. *Can you be sent to prison on your first offence?* she wondered wildly. What would her parents say when they found out?

But Dan was nodding his head as he listened, and he didn't seem in any hurry to pick up the phone and have them arrested. Instead, as Harry reached the end of the story, he looked hard at him. 'You should have called me,' he said.

'There wasn't time.'

'You didn't know that. This should have gone through the proper channels, Harry.'

'He'd have scarpered, you know he would.' Harry was frustrated. 'He was squatting, Dan.'

'That doesn't mean he doesn't value his possessions.'

'He didn't value the dog,' Lola put in, and then bit her tongue for speaking. But Harry flashed her an approving glance.

'He let us take the dog,' Harry pointed out.

Dan sighed. 'It's not that, Harry. I'm not so concern -ed about the criminal activities, though' – he flicked a look at Lola – 'you shouldn't get others involved. It's the personal safety aspect you haven't considered.'

'We're fine,' said Harry. Lola nodded, though she still felt shaky.

'That's not what I mean,' said Dan. 'He knows you both now. I don't want you getting into trouble with him.'

'I can handle it,' said Harry.

'Don't be stupid, Harry. If he's got a grudge . . .' Dan glanced at Lola and stopped abruptly. 'I'm saying it was an irresponsible thing to do.'

Lola was pale. *He knows our names!* she suddenly thought. *And he could guess we work here!* The world swam around her. 'Do you think,' she said faintly, 'he'd come after us . . . ?' She reached out for a shelf as nausea rose in her throat.

Harry grabbed her arm fiercely. 'Sit down. Sit on the floor.'

Lola sank to her knees, wondering if she was about to be sick. Harry crouched next to her, pushing the hair out of her face. 'Lola, can you hear me? It's going to be fine, I promise. Stay there a minute and you'll feel better.'

'Give her this,' came Dan's voice from far away.

There was movement above her, and then Harry pushed a plastic cup of water into her hand. 'Drink it.'

Slowly, the world came back into focus. Lola felt as though she were emerging from a dark tunnel, and the first thing she saw clearly was Harry's face. The look in his eyes took her aback. *He looks as though he really cares* . . . she thought muzzily.

'Lola,' he was saying, and his voice made her blink. 'Lola, I shouldn't have taken you with me. I'm sorry.' His hand brushed her hair out of her face again, and she felt vaguely surprised at its gentleness. 'But please don't worry. He's not going to come after us – didn't you see how relieved he was when we took the dog? I think he's more worried about being turned out of that house than anything else.'

'I'm taking this dog to the vet right now,' said Dan, breaking in on their conversation. 'She's dehydrated and needs fluids straight away.' He looked down at them, the dog in his arms, and his voice softened. 'Lola, you did the right thing. Please try not to worry

– you're safe here. You should try to take it easy this afternoon.'

Lola nodded, thankful that the nausea was going away. 'I haven't had lunch yet . . .'

Dan made a tutting noise. 'Harry, get Lola some food and make sure she stays warm. *You* might be hardened to this sort of thing, but she isn't.'

'No problem.'

'See you later,' said Dan, and the door banged behind him.

There was a small pause. Lola was suddenly aware just how close Harry was. If she looked up, she could practically count his eyelashes. The thought made her feel funny, so she kept her gaze on the floor. 'Thanks for the water,' she said eventually.

'Huh?' Harry seemed to be thinking of something else entirely. 'Oh – right. I'll get you some food. You want some soup?'

'Soup? Where from?'

'Maggie has some in the kitchen, I think.'

'Oh – yeah. OK.'

He nodded. 'Stay on the floor until you feel better.' Then he disappeared.

A few moments later, Naiha stuck her head into the office. 'What's going on?' she asked. 'Are you OK? Where've you been?'

Lola felt tired. 'Rescuing a dog,' she said flatly.

'What?' Naiha came into the office and pulled the door shut behind her. 'What dog, where?'

'That dog I told you about – the one in that awful house. And the man who didn't really live there – I mean, his dog, the one with the broken leg and . . .' To her shock, Lola discovered she was crying.

Naiha bent down to sit beside her, then saw the state of the carpet and thought better of it. Instead, she pulled one of the fleeces off the back of the door and spread it out on the floor before carefully lowering herself onto it. She put her arm around her friend. 'Lols, you're scaring me. What's going on?'

Between gulps, Lola tried to explain about the terrifying man who was squatting in the house, and about the state of the dog, not to mention the horrible stench of the house itself. 'And Dan said . . .' she hiccupped, 'that the man might come after us . . . and we said we'd tell the police . . . and Harry broke into the house!'

Naiha rolled her eyes. 'Why am I not surprised?'

Lola wiped her nose. 'Naiha, he was *amazing*. You can't imagine. He got down on the stinking floor to talk to the dog, and it just came to him, like – like magic!' She sniffed. 'And then when the man came in and I was so petrified, Naiha, like I couldn't move –

and Harry just stood up to him and told him he was breaking the law, and – and threatened him with all this stuff, and he just let us leave!'

'Wow.'

'I know!'

'You should go home,' Naiha said hopefully. 'You've had a shock. They can't argue with that. And I can come with you to make sure you're all right.'

Lola shook her head. 'No, I'm OK. Have you got a tissue?'

'No . . .'

'I'm all right now, it was just the shock. I don't need to go home.'

Naiha looked disappointed. 'Are you sure?'

'Yeah.'

'What about lunch? Shall I go down to the shop and get you something?' Naiha was obviously still looking for ways to avoid work.

'No, it's OK, Harry's getting me something. He's been really nice. A minute ago, I was practically fainting, and he got me a cup of water and—' she stopped abruptly. *I can't tell Naiha about him touching my face. It makes it sound as though he was trying to kiss me, and he wasn't, he was brushing my hair back but weirdly I can still feel where he touched me . . .*

'And what?' asked Naiha sharply. 'You've gone red. What happened?'

The door opened and Harry came in, holding a steaming mug. 'Oh, hi, Naiha. This is for Lola. Maggie only had one of those cup-a-soups left – they're a bit rank, but at least it's hot. No idea what flavour it is.'

'Thanks,' said Lola gratefully.

Harry nodded. 'I've got to get back to work.' His eyes narrowed. 'Let me know if you need anything, OK?'

Naiha waited until he had gone before commenting, '*Let me know if you need anything*?'

'He's just being nice.'

'So I see.'

Lola wrapped her hands around the mug. 'I can't figure him out, Naiha. There's all this stuff going on underneath, you know?'

'Mmm.' Her friend withdrew her arm from Lola's shoulders.

'He's really deep, I think.' Lola felt an urge to explain that there was more to Harry than dirt and DIY.

'Oh, come on, Lola, you're being so naïve.'

'What do you mean?'

'It's obvious. He's making a move on you.' Naiha's eyes narrowed. 'Or has he already done that?'

'Of course not!'

'You're blushing again! Did you get off with him before I came in?'

Lola's face burned. 'No!'

'Look, if you fancy him then just say so,' snapped Naiha. 'But it's not fair on Samir. He doesn't deserve to be cheated on.'

'I'm not cheating on Samir!' cried Lola.

'Well, good, because I can't understand why you'd dump him for someone like Harry. Samir is *miles* hotter than Harry!'

'For all I know, Samir's cheating on *me*,' said Lola.

'What? Oh, you mean that girl Sienna saw in Next. That doesn't mean anything, Lola, you know it doesn't.'

'You can't be sure,' argued Lola.

Naiha looked bewildered. 'But why would you even *look* at someone like Harry? He's dirty, he's scruffy and I bet he never brushes his teeth. Kissing him would be disgusting!'

'It's not just about the outside, Naiha! Harry's really kind and sweet underneath, and – and kissing him would *not* be disgusting!'

'Fine!' Naiha threw open the door to reveal Harry standing directly behind it, his face a picture of shock.

♥

Lola was so embarrassed that Harry had overheard her words that she avoided him all afternoon, which was harder than usual, since they were all supposed to be in the dog area. Fortunately, Naiha was in such a mood with her that Lola found it quite easy to work alone, grooming the long-haired dogs, checking the length of their toenails, refilling water bowls and helping Ian to give medicine to two dogs who were recovering from infections and were being kept in isolation. Harry took several more groups of dogs out for walks that afternoon and Lola ducked behind a nearby pen whenever he came into sight.

Dan came back and called Lola into his office to make sure she was all right. 'The vet thinks the dog you rescued will be OK,' he told her, 'but she's dehydrated so they can't operate on her broken leg yet.'

'When will we know – if she'll be OK?'

'We'll just have to wait – she's not a well animal at the moment, Lola.'

Lola nodded, biting her lip.

'But you did the right thing,' Dan said again, looking

her straight in the eye. 'You spotted an animal in distress and reported it to someone. It's just a shame that Harry took matters into his own hands.'

'I shouldn't have asked him. I should have come to you. It's my fault.'

'No,' said Dan, 'it isn't. Harry's – well – he's used to being independent, making decisions on his own.'

Lola hesitated. 'When we were out, he said something about being homeless.' She wasn't sure if she should be asking this, but somehow she wanted to know more about Harry. She twisted her fingers together. 'Has he . . . I mean, is he . . . homeless?'

'No!' Dan's reply came instantly. 'No, he's not homeless, Lola, don't worry about that. He has a home. It's just – not a very happy one.'

'Oh.'

Dan looked at her searchingly. 'I'll tell you a bit about him, so that you can see where he's coming from. He's got a lot of barriers up, but not without reason.'

Lola sat down. She felt strangely nervous, as though she were about to hear a great secret.

Dan put his hands together on the desk. 'Harry's been with us a while. He's made great progress but he comes from quite a troubled background. When he first started working here, he'd been excluded from school a few times because of fighting.' He saw her expression. 'He had a tutor at home, and they thought it would be good for him to be somewhere like this. I don't care how many exams people have failed. I just need them to work hard and listen properly. Harry took a while to understand that but now he's one of my best workers. He's got a real talent for handling dogs too – the kind of ability you don't see very often. Developing that has helped him turn a corner. He's back at school part-time, and he's not been in trouble for ages. But there'll always be that side to him – the side that takes risks and doesn't think about the consequences. I'm not saying it's an excuse for what he did, but it's why I'm not going to come down too hard on him. He feels very strongly about some things – taking care of animals being one of them.'

Lola wasn't sure what to say. 'Right.'

'I've told you this because I think it's good for people to see what the world is like for others,' said Dan. 'And also because I think you care. About Harry.'

Lola flushed. *Do I?* 'Yeah,' she mumbled, wondering what exactly Dan meant. Was he talking about caring in the friendly way? Or did he think she fancied Harry? What did *she* think herself? The squirming feeling in her tummy wasn't making it any clearer.

Dan smiled at her. 'We should have more news on the dog tomorrow.'

'Thanks.'

♥

That evening, summoned by text, Samir came round. 'Hey, gorgeous!' he said to Lola, pulling her into his arms. 'I've missed you so much!'

Lola kissed him back. 'Me too,' she replied, though something felt a bit odd. Normally, kissing him was fab, but today ... was he being less enthusiastic than usual? Had Naiha told him about Harry? Surely he wouldn't be kissing her at all if so ... 'Is everything OK?' she asked in a deliberately casual voice.

'Yeah, why?'

She shrugged. 'Oh, I dunno. Come on, let's go up to my room.'

Samir slumped onto her pink sofa when they got there. 'I am so beat! Working is a stupid idea!'

Lola smiled as she sat down next to him. 'What did you do today?'

'Till, stockroom, more till, more stockroom, yelled at by manager, called thick by a customer ...' Samir ticked them off on his fingers.

Lola was shocked. 'A customer called you thick? That's awful!'

'Yeah, it was because I couldn't find some minging trousers he wanted. I don't know. Next does about fifty different types of black trousers – how was I supposed to know which were the right ones?'

'He shouldn't have called you thick, though.'

'Yeah, my manager came up to me afterwards to make sure I was all right.' He grinned. 'But it was OK. Safi slipped a T-shirt into the customer's bag and he set off the security alarm at the door. They thought he was trying to steal it.' He started laughing. 'Apparently he was in their office for half an hour, arguing with them! They let him off with a warning.'

'Wow.' Lola tried to laugh. 'That Safi's kind of funny, then.'

'Yeah, she's cool. She's always playing tricks on people.' He shook his head admiringly. 'She comes up with stuff I'd never think of. And she gets away with it all the time!'

Lola's heart sank. Samir was obviously really keen on this Safi girl. She tried to change the subject. 'I did something mad today too.'

'You did? What?'

'I broke into a house.' Lola was surprised – that

wasn't quite what she'd meant to say, but somehow she felt she had to impress Samir.

It worked. Samir's jaw nearly hit the floor. His eyes bulged. 'You never!'

'I did! Well – actually, someone from the sanctuary did. He picked the lock. See, there was a dog inside and . . .' The story spilled out of Lola.

Samir listened, his eyes getting bigger and bigger. When Lola got to the part about the man coming in and catching them, he breathed, 'Wow!'

If Lola had hoped to take his mind off Safi, it worked. But not quite in the way she intended. 'And so,' she finished, 'Dan took the dog to the vet and hopefully she'll be all right. Though I'm really worried. She was so thin, Sam, her ribs were all sticking out.' Thinking of the dog, she felt her eyes well up. What if she died overnight? They would have rescued her too late . . .

Samir nodded. 'Do they do that kind of thing a lot, then?'

She was confused. 'What kind of thing? Who?'

'People at the sanctuary. Breaking into people's houses to rescue animals.' His eyes shone. 'Can I come? I so want to learn how to pick a lock! Did I ever tell you about the case my dad had? The burglar who could open anything? It was just so cool!'

Lola stared at him as Samir went into a long

description of the burglar's achievements. He hadn't realized she was upset about the dog at all. In fact, he didn't seem interested in the animal in the least – only in the criminal act of breaking into a house. She knew he loved pranks, but how could he miss the point so completely? She had the surreal feeling she could be screaming in his face and he wouldn't hear her. Mentally, she shook herself. This was *Samir*, good old Samir, cheerful popular gorgeous Samir – her *boyfriend*. So why did she feel like she didn't really know him?

And why, staring at the face of the hottest boy she knew, was she suddenly remembering Harry's touch on her cheek?

# Chapter 11

## do something that *means* something

Lola found it almost impossible to get to sleep that night. So many thoughts were dashing around her head: was the rescued dog going to die? Would the scary man, his angry face burned into her memory, come after her and Harry? To her surprise, Lola was more scared for Harry than she was for herself. Dan said he'd got into fights at school – what kind of fights? Were they the sort where you stood up for someone who was being picked on? Somehow Lola couldn't picture Harry standing up for another boy – not in the same way he'd defended an abused animal. Or did he get into fights because he was quick to anger; easy to wind up; against the world? Lola wasn't sure she could picture that either.

And why should it matter to her at all? Another two days and her work experience at the centre would be over. She wouldn't have to see Harry again. She could go back to normal life – school, family and Samir.

Samir. There was another thing bothering her. Why did she feel so fed up with him all of a sudden? He hadn't changed, had he? He was still cool and popular and fit. He was still the boy every girl wanted to go out with. She had been jealous of Safi, hadn't she? Even though Samir hadn't said he fancied her or anything . . . but then she'd told him the story of the dog and it was like he wasn't even *listening*. Why did Lola have the weirdest feeling that he wasn't the right boy for her any more?

*Maybe I've changed*, she wondered, and the thought was disturbing. *I don't want to change! Things were fine as they were! Besides, a person can't change in three days, that's just ridiculous.*

Sighing with frustration, Lola glanced at the clock. It was nearly 1 a.m. and she'd been lying awake for three hours. There was a tub of Ben and Jerry's ice cream in the freezer downstairs, wasn't there?

As soon as she'd had the thought, her stomach rumbled and she was out of bed and putting on her slippers. She wouldn't normally eat ice cream in the middle of the night, but this was an emergency. Milk wouldn't cut it this time.

There was indeed a tub of Ben and Jerry's Caramel Chew Chew in the freezer, but there was only a quarter of it left. *I might as well take it back upstairs with me.* She grabbed a spoon and the tub and started back up the stairs.

At the top of the stairs, she paused. There was that noise again. It was coming from Quinn's room, just like the night before. Lola tapped on the door softly.

The door opened a crack and Quinn peered out. In the dim light it was hard to see, but her eyes looked puffy. 'Oh, it's you,' she said in a whisper. 'You OK, Lola?'

'I'm fine. Are *you* OK?'

'Of course I—' Quinn started to say, but then she bit her lip. 'No, I'm not really. You can come in.'

'I brought ice cream,' suggested Lola helpfully.

Quinn shut the door behind them and smiled ruefully. 'I think I need more than ice cream.'

'Oh,' said Lola, not quite sure what her older sister meant by this. 'Uh . . . there's the drinks cabinet downstairs . . .'

Quinn shook her head. 'No, it's all right. I don't want anything really. Come and sit down.'

Lola looked around. Her sister may have left home a year ago, but Helena had kept Quinn's room exactly as it always was. There was a pale blue carpet and white walls edged with navy skirting. Navy curtains hung at the windows. It might have seemed boyish if it hadn't been for the floral stencilling around the room at waist height. Quinn's room had always felt extremely classy to Lola, who preferred pink butterflies and fluffy fairy lights to adorn her own room.

The four-poster bed with white curtains took up half of the floor, whilst a couple of squashy blue chairs and a dressing table occupied the other half. A door in the corner led to the *en suite* bathroom and the walk-in wardrobe. Quinn sat down in one of the blue chairs, a pile of used tissues scattered around its base.

Lola sat in the other, wondering what to say. She adored her sister, but Quinn lived away from home now, and there was a six-year age gap between them. They weren't as close as they had been. 'You've been crying,' she began gently. 'What's the matter, Quinn?'

Quinn reached for another tissue. 'I don't know if I can tell you. It's just too awful.'

Mad thoughts raced through Lola's head. Was Quinn pregnant? Had she committed a crime? Been dropped by her agency? 'I won't tell anyone.'

'All right. Here goes.' Quinn took a breath and then said, 'I hate modelling.'

At first, Lola thought she'd misheard. 'Pardon?'

'I hate modelling,' repeated Quinn. Her voice shook. 'I hate it, hate it – I don't want to do it any more!'

Lola was shocked. 'But I don't understand. You've always said you love modelling! We all love it!'

'*I* don't,' said Quinn more firmly.

'You've wanted to be a model since we were little,' pursued Lola, bewildered. 'We all played dressing up, and Dad used to come and do pretend photoshoots with us. And you're gorgeous – you're perfect for the job. You're tall and thin and you've got lovely hair and skin and . . . I know it's hard work. But you always said you loved it, that you didn't want to do anything else.'

Quinn pulled a face. 'Yeah, well, things have changed.'

'How?'

Quinn stared at the ice cream tub, as yet untouched, in Lola's hand. 'I can't eat that, you realize? In fact, I can't eat anything much at all these days. I am *constantly* hungry.'

'Why?'

'Because I have to stay skinny, stupid!' Quinn glared. 'Do you think I stay like this naturally?'

'I don't understand. We're all skinny in this family. I'm skinny, Sienna is skinny.'

'Not skinny enough. I'm a size eight, but loads of designers want thinner. I've been trying to get down to a size six.' She sighed. 'I'm just not sure it's worth it any more.'

'What about the agency? I mean, have they told you to lose weight?'

'No, not in so many words.' Quinn blew her nose again. 'But they do say things like "Editorial is so competitive at the moment" and "Of course, we don't approve of the way this campaign is run *but* . . ." I just feel under pressure the whole time.'

'Then don't do it. They'll have to take you as you are; you'll still get work. You're gorgeous.'

'Being gorgeous isn't enough,' said Quinn ruefully. 'But even when I do get work, I don't enjoy it like I used to. Everyone's so obsessed; it's like they're blinkered, they can only see their tiny part in the world. I have such boring conversations with people!'

'But what about the clothes? The photoshoots? The parties?'

Quinn gave a short laugh. 'Parties? I can live without them, Lola. They're all the same. People with a lot of money getting drunk. More boring conversations.'

'What about the celebrities?' Lola was trying to

understand why her sister would voluntarily give up her glamorous lifestyle.

'They're just *people*, Lola. And saying hello to someone is not the same as being their friend. What does it matter if Jessie J is in the same nightclub as me? I'm not going to sit down with her and have a cosy chat, am I?'

'Oh. Well, I guess not.'

'Look.' Quinn tucked her legs underneath her on the chair and pulled her dressing gown tightly around her. 'Standing around having your photo taken is fun to start with, but it's so tiring. And you're never wearing the right clothes either – the shoots for summer fashion take place in winter, so you're standing in a field freezing while they put a filter over the camera to make it look hot! And in the summer, you're standing by a stream in thirty-degree heat with a fur-lined parka on!'

'But—'

'And the catwalk shows are exhausting. Being pulled and pushed around, someone always doing your hair and your face. Putting clothes on, taking them off, and having to be cheerful all the time.'

'Oh, but surely—'

'Do you know what's the *most* annoying thing?'

'What?'

'No one ever wants to know what I think! I mean, sometimes these people dress me in stuff that is just *so* unflattering, and I want to say, no, not that belt, the buckle is in just the wrong place and it makes me look like I've got muffin tops when I haven't. And I overheard some people in a bar the other day talking about the situation in the Middle East, and they sounded so *clever*, Lola! Really intelligent; they were talking about power and dictators and whether democracy was really the right kind of society . . . And I felt so stupid, like I didn't know anything at all. I'd love to have conversations like that – well, any conversation really that wasn't just about looking beautiful.'

She looked down to see that she'd pulled a tissue to pieces in her outburst. 'I guess it's too late really. I'm a model now, and we're not supposed to have opinions or know about anything. We just have to stand there and look pretty. A man even said that to me last week, you know? I was talking about this local charity and how it was going to have to close because it didn't have any money. And he said, "Shut it, love, I pay you to stand there and look pretty, not lecture me about the way of the world."'

'That's so rude! You shouldn't put up with that.'

'And do what? Walk out? That's my *job*, Lola. He was right – he was paying me. I can't just walk out if I don't like the way I'm spoken to – word would get round and I'd never get any work!' Quinn shook her head. 'Oh, it's all such a mess!'

Lola bit her lip. She'd never heard Quinn talk like this before. Of course, their mother had always been frank with them about the harshness of the modelling world, but somehow Lola had always assumed she'd exaggerated the bad bits. And she'd certainly always thought that the good bits would be worth it. But the way Quinn was talking ... it didn't sound like much fun at all. Her big sister had got good grades at school; Lola knew she had brains as well as beauty. It must be frustrating not being able to use them; to always be judged on her looks. Lola was beginning to realize that she too was fed up with people seeing her as just a pretty face. Even Naiha dismissed her thoughts and ideas sometimes when they didn't fit in with her own. In fact, it was only at the sanctuary that people seemed to think she could be more than a daydreamer.

She looked at the ever-growing pile of tissues and felt so sorry for her sister. Getting up, she gave her a hug. 'What are you going to do?'

'I don't know. I can't exactly tell Mum, can I?' Quinn started to cry again. 'She's always been so supportive of my career, and she bought me that flat and the car, and she's always so excited when I get a new contract. She loves telling people her daughter's a successful model like she was – how can I take that away from her?'

'But it's not her life, it's yours. I'm sure she'd understand . . .' Lola trailed off uncertainly and sat back. *Would* their mother understand? When it was everything she'd trained her girls to do? Helena had spent thousands of pounds over the years on the girls – spray tans, manicures, pedicures, drama lessons, photoshoots, facials, haircuts, highlights . . . If Quinn gave up modelling, wouldn't all of that have been a waste? A quiet voice in her head was also adding, *What if you decide you don't want to be a model either? Will Mum think all her daughters are letting her down?*

Quinn took a breath and tried to control herself. 'I can't tell her, can I? You know what she's like. She lives for fashion – and now she can't do the mainstream stuff herself she sort of lives through me.'

There was a pause. 'If you're not enjoying it any more, then you shouldn't do it,' said Lola lamely. She felt like she wasn't being much help.

Quinn sighed. 'I know. But what else can I do?' She looked at Lola with big, brimming eyes.

Lola gave her another hug. 'You'll find something. It'll be OK.'

Quinn pulled back to gaze into her face. 'Don't go into modelling,' she said urgently. 'It doesn't *mean* anything. Do something that *means* something.'

Lola smiled. 'Hey, my other career idea is a fashion designer.'

'That's even worse!'

Lola's face fell.

Quinn went on quickly, 'I'm sorry, I didn't mean that. I suppose – I'm just disillusioned with the whole thing. Fashion, photography, magazines – everything. When you've seen it from the inside, you do wonder what it's all about really.'

'But I love designing,' said Lola.

Her sister gave her a small smile. 'Then you should be a designer. But there are other things to do than fashion. Just – don't forget that.'

'OK.' Quinn looked so serious that it gave Lola a pang of uncertainty. Not design clothes and bags and shoes? But what else was there? She picked up the tub of ice cream. 'Oh, yuck, it's completely melted.'

'I like it like that,' said Quinn wistfully.

'You have it, then.' Lola held it out. 'I don't want it any more.'

'Oh, I can't.'

'Yes you can.'

Quinn smiled at her. 'Thanks, sis. Hey, maybe tomorrow night you can tell me all *your* worries.'

Lola smiled back at her. 'That sounds good.'

# Chapter 12

## I really, really want to kiss Harry

'I'm going to pick up your dog later,' Dan told Lola when she arrived. He was smiling. 'The vet says she's done really well overnight. He's going to set the bone this morning and says we can care for her here. Morning, Naiha.'

Lola turned as Naiha came into the office, rubbing her eyes groggily. 'Hey. You OK?'

'Yeah.' Naiha didn't smile. She put her bag on the usual shelf. 'What are we doing today?'

'Rabbits,' said Dan promptly. 'You're back with Ruth today. And I'll come and get you, Lola, when I've picked up the dog from the vet. I'm assuming you'd like to see her?'

'Oh, yes – please, I'd love to.'

The two girls headed over to the rabbit barn. Lola knew her friend was in a bad mood; it was written all over Naiha's face. 'What's going on? Are you OK?'

'I'm fine. I'm just really knackered. I had a late night.'

'Oh. Did you go out?' For a moment, Lola felt hurt. Why hadn't Naiha invited her?

'Only to my cousin's. My aunt rang up in a panic and said she'd run out of coriander and she couldn't leave the kids to go to the shop and blah blah. So Mum and I went round and ended up staying half the night.' Naiha screwed up her eyes. 'It's really bright today.'

Lola glanced up at the weak February sun. 'It's no brighter than yesterday.'

'Well, it looks bright to me,' snapped Naiha.

Lola waited a moment before asking, 'Did you have a good time, though?'

'Yeah, it wasn't too bad in the end. My third cousin Hasan is staying with them.'

'The fit one you met last year?'

'Yeah.' Naiha grinned. 'He is *well* hot, Lola.'

'Did you – did you kiss him?'

Naiha looked smug. 'Just a bit.'

'Wow.' Lola felt pleased for her friend. 'So are you going out with him then?'

'He's only staying with my aunt for a bit, while his dad finds a new flat. They're moving out of the family home.' Naiha flapped her hand in the air. 'Separation, divorce or something. All a bit messy. But I said we could go out on a double date. You and Samir and me and Hasan.'

'Yeah.' Lola tried to sound enthusiastic. 'That would be fab.'

Naiha looked hard at her. 'That is, if you're still going out with Samir . . .'

'Of course I am,' said Lola uncertainly. *But I don't want to, do I? Or do I?*

By now they had reached the rabbit barn, and Ruth soon put them to work cleaning out the rabbit cages, just as they had on Monday. Naiha's grumpy mood returned and she flung the mop around, prompting a reminder from Ruth to handle the rabbits gently.

Lola stayed out of her friend's way as much as possible. She was conscious of a strong wish to see Harry. *Stop it!* she told herself. *Why would you want to see him? He's not even a friend!* But even so, every time someone came into the barn, her heart thudded in case it was him.

By the time Dan came to fetch her, Lola felt as though she might explode with the tension. 'Lola! You can come and see the dog now,' Dan called.

'Go,' said Ruth, smiling. She'd heard the story of the rescue and thoroughly approved. 'And why don't you go straight to lunch afterwards? Naiha and I can finish up here.'

Naiha glowered. Lola felt guilty about leaving

Naiha to do her work, but she was desperate to see the dog. Naiha wouldn't understand, but then she hadn't made an effort to, had she? Lola was beginning to find her best friend was getting on her nerves big time. Leaving her mop and bucket, she practically ran to the indoor isolation area. 'Go quietly,' Dan had told her. 'Ill animals need peace and calm.'

Lola carefully opened the main door and went inside. She was instantly struck by the temperature. The rest of the sanctuary might be bearing the brunt of winter, but the heating was on full blast in here. Her fingers tingled with the sudden warmth.

To her right was a long low counter, backed by storage shelves. Medicine kits were visible on the shelves, along with bottles and instructions for administering doses on the walls. To the left was a row of cages on the floor, each big enough for a large dog, containing straw, newspaper and soft bedding. In the third cage, a small dog lay on a blue blanket and Lola's heart turned over.

The dog was even smaller than she remembered – or maybe it was because half her fur had been shaved away leaving bare patches. It was warm in here but still the dog gave an occasional tremble. Now that Lola could see her properly, it was heartbreaking. The matted fur had gone to reveal two or three cuts that had been stitched up, and her right hind leg was wrapped in plaster from toe to hip. Her head lay on her front paws, but as Lola took a step forward, the dog started in fright, jerking up from the bed with a small yelp.

'Ssh,' said Lola softly. 'It's me, Lola. Hello, sweetie. Do you remember me?' She lifted the lid to the cage and put her hand in for the dog to sniff it. After a moment, the dog relaxed and allowed Lola to stroke her. She was terribly thin, but her eyes were bright, and Lola suddenly found that tears were streaming down her face. She was so relieved that the dog was still alive and that they hadn't been too late. 'No matter what happens,' she whispered to the dog, 'I'm glad we came to find you.'

'So am I,' said a quiet voice behind her, making her jump in shock. Harry had come in without making a sound.

Lola scrabbled to wipe her face, embarrassed that he'd caught her crying. 'Oh – hi. I – er . . . I just came in to see how she's doing.'

'Yes, Dan told me,' Harry said simply. 'Are you all right?'

'Yes, yeah, I'm fine. I just . . .' To her horror, Lola couldn't stop the tears. They kept on coming, streaming down her face and dripping onto the floor. *My mascara must be running everywhere! And I haven't even got a tissue!* 'Sorry.'

'That's all right,' said Harry, as though it didn't matter to him at all. 'You are allowed to cry over animals.'

'Yes,' choked Lola, 'but I look awful.'

Harry gave a snort. 'Why would that matter?' Shaking his head, he bent to lift the little dog out of the cage.

Lola wiped her face on her sleeve again. 'I feel really ugly, that's all.'

Harry stroked the dog. '*She* doesn't care. Besides, there are more important things than how you look.'

'I know that,' said Lola defensively.

'The important thing,' went on Harry, his gaze softening as he looked at the dog in his arms, 'is that this little girl is recovering all right. She's had enough upset in her life. She needs looking after and treating well.' He glanced at Lola. 'Do you want to hold her?'

'Can I?'

'Of course. Sit down over here.' He indicated a place against the wall. Lola shuffled into it and held out her arms. Gently, Harry passed the dog to her. The little body trembled in her arms.

'She's so light!'

He settled himself beside her. 'She's underweight.

The vet reckons she hasn't been fed properly for months.'

Lola tried to adjust her arm so that she wasn't touching the plastered leg. 'How long will it take for this leg to heal?'

'A few weeks.'

'How – how did it break?'

He shot her a look. 'Kicked, probably. Or hit with something.'

Lola nodded, not trusting herself to speak.

'Would you rather I lied to you?' asked Harry, his voice soft. 'Do you want me to tell you she fell off a wall or something?'

'No.' Lola bent to the dog in the hope that she could hide her face. The dog whimpered slightly.

'She's been badly treated,' said Harry in a whisper. 'But the vet says her spirit isn't broken. She'll make a great pet for someone. She's . . . um . . .' He cleared his throat. 'He said she's got a lot of love to give.'

'Oh.' Lola felt her cheeks suddenly flame. It was kind of embarrassing to hear Harry say the word 'love', even though she knew he was talking about the dog. There was an awkward silence. Lola cast around desperately for something to say. 'Um . . . so, do you have any pets at home?' *Dan said he has a home, so it must be all right to ask about it.*

Harry seemed grateful for the change of subject and replied hastily, 'No, no, I don't. We used to have a cat but it got run over.'

'I'm sorry.'

'Yeah. It was horrible. I saw it happen too.' He shuddered. 'Gave me nightmares for months.'

'You didn't get another cat?'

'Nah. There's no one at home who really cares about animals except me.' He rubbed the back of his neck. 'My parents don't care about much really.'

Lola had guessed this from what Dan had told her, but the casual way Harry said it shocked her. 'What do you mean?'

Harry opened his mouth to answer and then shrugged. 'It doesn't matter.'

She glanced at him. He looked strangely young again, like the time he had coaxed the shivering dog out from behind the sofa. She found herself wanting to know more. 'You can tell me,' she said. 'I'm not going to laugh or anything.'

He looked at her. 'I know you wouldn't laugh. It's just – all right, then. They drink, OK? Well, my dad does. A lot. He's out most of the time with his mates. My mum's depressed so she can't work. She sits around at home all day and when Dad comes home he shouts about the state of the house and she cries, and . . .' He shrugged resignedly again. 'And so it's not like they notice me much. Let alone a cat.'

Lola was appalled. 'That sounds really bad. What does your dad do?'

'Nothing. He's unemployed. He drinks the benefits money.'

'Oh.'

He glanced at her and laughed. 'You have no idea what sort of life I have. You probably come from a lot of money – big house, big car . . . am I right?'

Lola coloured. 'Yes.' She'd never felt like she had to defend her family before. 'But my parents have worked for it. I mean, I don't get everything I ask for, you know. I'm not spoilt.'

He raised an amused eyebrow. 'Really?'

'I'm not! I get told off, like everyone else. I get – uh – sent to my room. And just because I've got loads of stuff it doesn't mean I'm happy all the time. I argue with my sister. You know – ordinary stuff.'

'Ordinary stuff,' repeated Harry, still with that amused light in his eyes.

Lola felt slightly uncomfortable. 'We're just normal people,' she said, though it sounded lame to her. She looked at him, sitting there with that thoughtful expression, strangely vulnerable, for all his self-confidence. 'Maybe I should be more like you,' she said without thinking, and nearly died of embarrassment.

'More like me? How?'

'Oh, I just meant . . . well, maybe I do live in a bit of a bubble sometimes. Having loads of things. Maybe I forget sometimes that other people don't have them.'

He nodded. 'This place must be a bit of a shock for you.'

'It is,' she admitted. 'I knew there were people who looked after animals. And I knew animals were badly treated and all that. But I guess I thought that charities had big warm buildings and lots of paid staff to run them, and I never imagined you'd have to mend your own fences and stuff like that.'

'You watch too much TV.'

'Yeah – that's probably where I got it all. *Animal Rescue* and stuff like that. I never thought about where you'd put the animals nobody wanted – well, I never thought about it at all.'

He picked at his thumb. 'What do you think now?'

'Not sure. I suppose I've been a bit surprised that people choose to work here,' she said honestly. 'I mean, it's not very nice work. And you're dirty the whole time. But then I suppose you still get paid.'

'Not much,' he said. 'I get a bit, but people like Maggie have been here for years and they're still on minimum wage.'

'How much is minimum wage?'

He told her.

Lola's eyes widened. 'But that's – that's a tiny amount!'

'They do it because they love the animals.' Harry squinted at his thumb.

'Are you all right?'

'Just a splinter.'

'Let me have a look.' Lola reached out for his hand. 'I'm good at splinters – got long nails.' The dog shifted comfortably in her lap and went back to sleep.

Harry let her take his hand. 'I got it off a fence post. It's not that bad.'

The skin on his thumb was red and inflamed. 'This looks really sore,' said Lola. 'When did you do it?'

'Can't remember.'

'Hold still.' Lola peered at his thumb. The light wasn't very good but she didn't want to move while the dog was still asleep. Carefully, she pulled her nail across the area.

'Ow!'

'I see it.' The top of the splinter showed in the dim light, embedded in the pad of the thumb. 'Hang on.'

Harry pulled a face as she squeezed the area. 'Your nails are sharp,' he complained.

'That's the point.'

His lips pressed together as though he were determined not to cry out. Lola dug her nail into the side of the splinter and eased it out. 'There!' She held it up. 'Look how long it was!' Then she realized Harry was staring at her. 'What?'

His face was so close she could practically count his freckles. His eyes gazed straight into hers, and there was something curious in them, as though he were trying to figure her out. Lola swallowed. She could feel his breath on her face, and for some unaccountable reason her heart was suddenly beating twice as fast. *I've never felt like this with Samir . . . I really, really want to kiss Harry.* The thought flashed into her head and made her blink with alarm. The dog snorted as she flinched.

Harry saw her recoil and flushed, getting to his feet immediately. 'Thanks, then,' he said gruffly. 'For getting the splinter out. Uh – do you want help getting the dog back into the cage?'

'No, no, I'm sure I can do it,' Lola said hastily, avoiding his eyes. *I can't believe I nearly kissed him! What came over me?*

'All right,' he said, and left, the door clicking shut behind him.

Lola struggled to her feet. It would have been much easier to have help, but she would rather eat her own hair than call Harry back. With difficulty, she placed the dog in her cage, stroking her gently. The dog licked her hand and settled on the blue blanket.

Lola stared at it. *It was just a mistake*, she told herself firmly. *It's warm in here and you got a bit emotional. Stop thinking about Harry, go back to your normal life and DON'T make things complicated!*

♥

'You're so quick at this now,' Ruth said, smiling at the two girls as they cleaned the cages. 'You'll be finished in no time.'

Lola smiled back at her, feeling proud. Ruth was a sweet person and it felt good to help out – it obviously meant a lot to her.

Naiha winced. 'My back hurts.'

'Does it?'

'Yeah, just – aaah! Ow, ow!' Naiha bent over, her face screwed up in pain.

Ruth jumped up and went to help her. 'Come and sit down over here.'

'It's all right,' said Naiha, sitting down gingerly. 'It's just about *there*, you know. It really hurts. I think I pulled something.'

'Can you straighten up?' asked Ruth.

'I, maybe – ow! No, I can't.'

Ruth threw a look at Lola. 'I think Naiha should sit down for a bit. Can you handle the rest of the cleaning?'

'Yeah, of course,' said Lola, worried. She came over to grab her friend's hand. 'You all right, Naiha?'

Naiha gave her a valiant smile. 'Yeah, I'm sure I will be in a minute. When it stops . . . ooh.' She winced again.

Lola grimaced in sympathy. 'If it's really bad, I could give Corin a call. He's got physiotherapists at the club.'

Naiha waved the suggestion away. 'No, no, I just need to rest. Thanks, though.'

'OK.' Lola got back to work.

'Let us know if you need anything,' Ruth said as she too went back to her jobs.

Lola was trying not to think about Harry, but she couldn't help replaying the recent scene in her mind. What would have happened if she'd kissed him? Would he have kissed her back? *I looked awful*, she remembered. *All that mascara running down my face. But Harry hardly seemed to notice.*

She was so busy trying to block him from her mind that when he came into the rabbit barn it was a total shock. Lola swung round to see him in conversation with Ruth, a hammer and nails in his hands. Then he looked up and caught her eye, and both of them flamed red and looked away quickly. Ruth turned to see what Harry had been looking at, and her mouth twitched into a smile.

Naiha hadn't missed the exchange either, and her eyes narrowed. When Harry left, she called out to Lola, '*Now* tell me you don't fancy him.'

Lola flushed again, glancing at Ruth in embarrassment. 'It's not like that.'

'Yeah, yeah. You can't fool me, Lola. You don't know where to look when he's around. Wanting a re-match of your snogfest in the office, are you?'

Ruth raised an inquiring eyebrow.

'It wasn't a snogfest,' said Lola defensively. 'We didn't even kiss.'

Naiha rolled her eyes. 'You are such a liar! It's written all over your face! *And* his! Look at the way he blushed just now!'

Lola didn't reply. She felt angry with Naiha for embarrassing her in front of Ruth like that. She bit her lip as she reached down to roll up some more newspaper.

Ruth watched her for a moment and then came over. Bending down next to Lola, she said in a low voice, 'I know it's none of my business, but if there is something going on, then I'm glad.'

Lola glanced at her, surprised.

Ruth smiled. 'Harry's got so many barriers up, it'd be good to see someone break through them. He's such a nice boy underneath it all, but he hasn't had many people care about him.'

'Oh.' Lola looked at the ground again, feeling something flutter in her stomach.

'You seem like a really nice girl too,' said Ruth, still keeping her voice low. 'Maybe you'd be good for Harry.'

'Mmm.' Lola didn't know what else to say, but to her relief Ruth had obviously finished. She gave Lola another smile and then moved away.

Behind them, Naiha stood up and said loudly, 'I am *so* bored of this place.' It was as though she had realized she wasn't getting any attention.

'Is your back better?' asked Ruth sharply, noticing that Naiha had removed her hand from her hip.

'My what?' asked Naiha innocently. 'Oh, my back? You didn't really believe I'd hurt it, did you?'

'What?' Lola put the sodden newspaper she was holding into the bucket. 'You were making it up?'

Naiha grinned. 'Can't believe you both fell for it, actually. Come *on*, who wants to be clearing up poo all day? I fancied a bit of time off, that's all.' She looked from one to the other. 'Oh, you can't be serious. I was just kidding around.'

'While we did all the work,' said Lola in a low tone. All of a sudden she was furious. 'You fancied a *bit of time off*? What about *us*?'

'What *about* you?' Naiha stared back, challenging. 'You have plenty of time off, don't you? Rescuing dogs, nursing sick animals – you're a regular saint, aren't you? Or is it all so you can sneak off to meet up with Harry?'

'This has nothing to do with him!' Lola cried. 'You're just being a lazy—'

'Working here is about teamwork,' Ruth broke in. 'There's a lot to do. It's only fair that we share it equally.'

'Yeah, well, I'm not part of your "team", am I?' Naiha said, making speech marks in the air. 'I'm just here because my stupid school put me here, and you know what? I've had enough.'

'What do you mean?'

'I'm going,' said Naiha, pulling off her gloves and slapping her hands together. 'I'm out of here.'

'But we're here till the end of tomorrow,' said Lola, unable to believe she was hearing this.

'*You're* here till the end of tomorrow,' Naiha said, jabbing a plum-coloured fingernail in Lola's direction. '*I'm* off to catch a bus into town for some serious retail therapy.'

'You're leaving us to go *shopping*?' asked Ruth, her pixie face pale.

'Best thing to do when you need cheering up,' Naiha told her. 'You could benefit from a bit of a fashion update yourself, Ruth. Didn't anyone tell you stonewashed jeans went out with the last century?'

Lola glanced at Ruth's face, which was pink with humiliation. 'Naiha, you're being mean.'

'I'm just saying it like it is.' Naiha crossed her arms, unrepentant. It was almost as though, having started, she couldn't stop. 'Some people just don't make the best of themselves. I'd start with your hair, personally.'

Ruth touched a shaking hand to her neck. 'My hair?'

'Yeah. You look like you've stuck your finger in an electric socket,' said Naiha, miming someone getting an electric shock. 'Ker-pow! Albert Einstein hair.'

Ruth looked at the floor. Lola noticed that there were tears in her eyes. 'That's enough,' Lola said sharply. 'You're way out of line.'

'Yeah? I haven't even got started on *you* yet.'

'Don't bother.'

Naiha stared at her for a moment, then gave a sarcastic laugh. 'You know what? I won't. I can't even remember why I *bothered* being friends with you. Friends don't keep secrets from each other, and they don't *lie*. So, see you around, Lola.' Casting a last contemptuous look at Ruth, she stalked out of the barn.

There was an awkward pause. 'I'm so sorry,' Lola said at last. 'She shouldn't have said any of that. Are you all right?'

Ruth took a breath. 'Yeah, I'm OK. I've had worse.' She flicked a glance at Lola. 'Are *you* OK?'

Lola sighed. 'Yeah. Me and Naiha – it's kind of an up-and-down friendship.' *More downs than ups at the moment*, she thought. It was hard to remember why exactly they were friends in the first place.

'Thing is,' said Ruth, 'I'd like to spend more money on clothes. Or my hair – or anything, really. I cut it myself, you know.'

'Oh,' said Lola, biting her tongue to prevent herself saying yes, she'd guessed.

'I just haven't got enough for a haircut. And it's only hair, isn't it? I mean, it doesn't *matter*.'

Lola shuffled, uncomfortably aware of how much she – or rather her mother – spent on her own expensive haircuts and highlights. 'Of course it doesn't matter,' she said reassuringly, though the words almost hurt her.

'Working here doesn't pay much,' said Ruth hesitantly. 'But if we were paid more, we couldn't look after so many animals. I'm not more important than them.' Her gaze softened as she looked at a nearby pen, where three rabbits were nibbling contentedly at a pile of dandelion leaves. 'I don't need those things – haircuts, new clothes – not really. I'd rather these little guys were happy.'

'Yeah, I can see that.' Lola hesitated. 'It doesn't have to cost, you know. You can do a lot with what you've already got.'

'What do you mean?' Ruth was curious.

'Well, the jeans, for example. You could put a couple of patches on them – or dye them a darker colour. Or do some stitching up the side of the legs, to make them look a bit different. If you wanted to, that is.'

Ruth smiled. 'I'm not very good at that kind of thing. Do you like sewing?'

'Yes – yes, I do, actually. Art and textiles are my

favourite lessons at school. I think maybe I'd like to be a fashion designer when I grow up.' As she said it, Lola remembered her sister's words. *Do something that means something*, she'd said. Maybe this was an opportunity? 'Would you – do you want me to have a go for you? At your jeans, I mean. Only if you wanted . . .'

Ruth's eyes lit up. 'Would you? That would be so kind of you! I wouldn't know where to start, but I love pretty things.'

Lola nodded. 'Sure. If you bring me a couple of things tomorrow, I'll see what I can do with them.'

Ruth was beaming now. 'You know, I felt on the first day that you were more likely to fit in here than Naiha. Some people have very closed-off minds. But you're different, you've got such a kind side to you, really considerate. And you haven't complained about the work either, not like some people. And look at what you did yesterday, rescuing that poor little dog! No wonder Harry likes you.'

Lola flushed at the praise and mumbled something.

Dan stuck his head into the barn. 'What's going on? Naiha just came to get her bag. Is she on a break?'

'I think she's left,' said Ruth.

'Left?'

'Walked out. She – er – she said she'd had enough.'

'Oh. Oh, I see.' Dan stood still. Then he sighed. 'I'm not really surprised. She didn't like it here at all. It's out of her comfort zone. I'd better ring the school.' He glanced at Lola. 'You're still here, though?'

'Yes.'

He gave her a warm smile. 'Excellent.'

*Yes*, thought Lola. *I'm still here – and why? It's cold, and the work is hard . . .*

*But I don't walk out on things. I won't. Not when people need me.*

# Chapter 13

## you don't have to if you don't want to

It felt strange to be collecting her bag and walking to the gates on her own at the end of the day. Lola wondered whether Naiha really had gone shopping. She was so angry with her. Naiha had seen how hard people worked here, and yet she'd walked out. Not only that, she'd been horribly rude to poor Ruth – and even called Lola a liar! It wasn't the first time the two of them had argued, but the way Lola was feeling right now she wouldn't be calling Naiha any time soon. If ever. *How can I be friends with someone so mean?* she thought. *I'd better call Tasha later and tell her what happened, before Naiha can make it sound like my fault.* She wondered if her other friends would take sides when they were all back at school. Things could get really nasty.

She was so busy thinking about Naiha that she

almost walked straight into Harry, who was digging up a large stone in the driveway. 'Oh – sorry!'

He straightened up. 'That's OK.' Was he blushing again? Lola couldn't be sure, the low winter sun was in her eyes. 'I can't get this bu— er, this stone out.'

'Why do you need to dig it up?'

'It catches all the cars that drive up here. Dan said someday someone will drive over it and their windscreen will crack, or their suspension will go, and we'll have to pay costs because we own the land. I promised I'd try to get it out.'

'Aren't you supposed to be going home?'

He shrugged. 'Yeah, at some point.'

'Got too much work?'

He rubbed his arm over his face and scuffed his shoe against the rock. 'My brother's home at the moment,' he said. 'We don't get on.'

'Oh. Is he older than you?'

'Yeah. He got sacked last week and his mate kicked him out and now he's back on the dole and lazing around the house getting mad at everyone. He and my dad go out drinking together. I try to avoid them as much as I can.'

'I see.'

Harry shrugged. 'It's all right. I'll grab some crisps

or something from the shop and go back later. Best not to get in their way.'

'Crisps? What, for dinner?'

'Yeah. It's that or beans on toast and I've had those three days running now.'

Lola stared at him. Crisps for dinner? She thought guiltily of Corin's lovingly prepared meals, and before she knew what she was saying, she blurted out, 'Why don't you come to dinner at my house?'

Harry's eyes widened. 'What, now? Today?'

'Yes, why not?' Lola knew her face was reddening but she couldn't back out now. 'Please come.'

'Oh – well . . .' Harry glanced up towards the office.

'You're meant to be going home, you said. This rock will wait till tomorrow. And – and tomorrow's my last day.' *Why did I say that?*

Harry caught her gaze and held it. 'Are you sure?'

'Yes. It'll be fun.' Lola's fingers were tingling, and she clenched her fists. *I'm just asking him home for tea*, she told herself sternly. *This does not mean I fancy him.* She ignored the faint worry about Samir. Should she really be inviting Harry home when she already had a boyfriend? *But it's not like that*, she mentally added. *I'm asking him because I feel sorry for him, because otherwise he won't get any dinner apart from crisps.*

Harry smiled. 'All right. Thanks.'

Corin was surprised when Lola told him she'd invited Harry back to their house, but he was friendly enough. Harry's jaw dropped when he slid into the back of Corin's Audi. Lola noticed he was careful not to put his dirty hands on the seats, tucking them into his pockets instead. 'Do you like cars, Harry?' asked Corin.

Harry nodded. 'Yeah. My neighbour's doing up an old MG. I help out sometimes.'

'If you could have any car, what would it be?'

'A Range Rover Sport,' Harry said without hesitation.

Corin whistled through his teeth. 'Nice.'

'I saw it on *Top Gear*,' Harry added.

'Sienna loves that programme,' Lola told him. 'Oh – my younger sister. She's twelve. You'll see her when we get home. And my older sister Quinn too, she's home from London for a bit. The one who's a model.'

'Oh, right.' Harry looked a bit startled.

It wasn't long before they were pulling into the driveway and parking up by the front door. Lola's heart thudded in her chest. What would Harry make of her family? What would *they* make of *him*? Suddenly she wasn't so sure this was a good idea. But it was too late now.

Corin was already opening the front door and

showing Harry in. Lola followed, nearly walking straight into Harry for the second time in half an hour. He had stopped dead in the hallway, gazing up in stupefaction. 'Jeez.'

Lola looked upwards. The hall was the tallest room in the house, stretching right up to the top floor. A chandelier dangled above their heads. There was nothing odd about it to her eyes, but obviously it was something Harry wasn't used to. She bit her lip. If he was going to be freaked out by the hallway, what on earth would he think of the rest of the house?

Corin threw his keys onto the hall table and went through to the sitting room, where Lola heard a murmur of voices.

'Are you OK?' she asked Harry awkwardly.

'What? Oh – yeah. Yeah, I'm fine. You *live* here?' He shook his head. 'It's like a footballer's mansion or something.'

Sienna suddenly appeared in the doorway, her eyes alight with curiosity. She was wearing a lilac babydoll dress with black hotpants and ballet pumps. Her gaze swept over Harry with something like astonishment. 'Hello.'

Harry blinked. 'Blimey, she looks just like you.'

Lola grinned. 'This is Sienna, my little sister. Remember I was telling you about her?'

'Yeah. Hi.'

'This is Harry,' added Lola.

'Hi, Harry,' said Sienna. 'So – er – you work with Lola, right? At the sanctuary?' Lola knew exactly what she was thinking: *Who is this scruffbag and why has Lola brought him home? He'll drop mud on the carpet!*

Harry seemed to have the same thought at the same moment. He looked down at his feet. 'Oh – I'd better take these off, right?'

'That's all right,' said Sienna, and giggled suddenly. 'It doesn't matter. Come through to the sitting room.' She ran ahead, obviously dying to tell the others.

Harry hesitated for a moment and shot Lola a look. Impulsively, she said, 'You don't have to if you don't want to. Was this a really bad idea?'

His expression relaxed at her words and he grinned. 'Nah, this is fun. I can pretend I'm a millionaire.'

Lola grinned back. 'All right. I promise I won't let my family eat you alive.'

'I'm not all that tasty,' said Harry, and instantly looked appalled at his own words.

Lola wanted to giggle like Sienna, but she squashed the feeling. Harry was actually in her house! It was like the world turned on its head!

Helena got up from the sofa in one easy moment,

extending her hand towards Harry so he had no choice but to shake it. 'Lovely to meet you,' she said, her eyes sweeping across him as Sienna's had done, but this time with professional appreciation. 'My goodness, what lovely cheekbones you have.'

'Er . . . thanks,' said Harry.

'Is Quinn here?' asked Lola.

Her mother's expression, always serene, seemed to stiffen slightly. 'She's upstairs.'

*She's told her*, Lola thought to herself. *Quinn's told Mum she doesn't want to be a model any more.* From the steely look in her mother's eyes, Lola suspected she hadn't taken it well. However, there was nothing but kind interest in the way she took Harry under her wing, asking him if he'd like a drink and making him comfortable. *My mother may have mixed with the rich and famous*, thought Lola, *but she knows how to make anyone feel at home*.

Harry, a ginger beer in one hand, relaxed a little on the sofa as Helena told him about the two cats she'd had whilst growing up – 'and a hamster called Snowball that escaped one night and was never seen again.'

Sienna, whilst staring hard at Harry with a curiosity Lola found almost rude, took the opportunity to remind Helena just how much she wanted a pet. 'And

Lola wants one too, don't you, Lola? She's scared of big dogs but she wants a toy one. A Pomeranian.'

Harry looked surprised. 'Really?'

Lola flushed. 'I don't want a Pomeranian any more.'

'But they're so cute!'

'Yes, but there are other cute dogs too.' Lola found herself thinking of the dog they'd rescued. No one could call her cute, but there was something so appealing about the vulnerable look in her eyes.

'Besides, it's more about spirit than appearance . . .' added Harry, catching her eye.

Lola smiled. *He knew exactly what I was thinking! That's amazing!*

Her mother's sharp eyes had missed nothing of this. 'Lola, why don't you go and see if Quinn wants to come down? Better yet, take Harry up with you; show him around if you like. You lot could all get into the pool while you're waiting for dinner.'

Sienna jumped up. 'Cool! I feel like a swim. I'll see you down there!'

'Er . . .' said Harry.

Lola nodded towards the door. 'You coming?' She smiled, faintly embarrassed. 'You can have the guided tour if you like.'

'OK.'

The two of them made their way upstairs. Lola wanted to point out things to him as they went, but she felt strangely tongue-tied. Her own house seemed so big all of a sudden; so extravagant. She wondered what Harry's house was like but didn't dare ask. Harry whistled softly at his surroundings and then fell silent. *I'd give anything to know what he's thinking.*

She hesitated outside Quinn's door but decided to leave it until last. 'This way.'

Harry couldn't hold back an astonished, 'Whoa!' at the family bathroom, with its roll-top bath in the middle of the room directly under the skylight; its gold taps and the two basins side by side. Fluffy white towels hung over the gold towel rail. He ran his hand over the side of the bath, shaking his head in awe. 'This is *amazing*. Oh . . .' His hand had left a dirty smudge on the white enamel.

'That's OK,' said Lola hastily. 'I'll wash it off.'

'Maybe I'll just wash my hands,' Harry said, reaching for the perfumed soap on the side of the basin. Lola handed him a towel when he'd finished. 'Thanks. Now my hands smell of – what *is* that?'

'*Honey I Washed The Kids* soap,' said Lola. 'It's from Lush.'

'From where?'

'Lush. Oh, never mind. It's my favourite soap shop.'

'You have a favourite *soap* shop?' asked Harry in disbelief.

'Yes, but they don't just do soap, they do—' She stopped. 'You're teasing me.'

He grinned. 'Just a bit. You have to admit it's a bit – well, mad. Soap is soap, isn't it?'

'That's what *you* think.' She grinned back at him. 'Have you finished gawping at the bathroom?'

'Yeah, I need something else to gawp at now.'

*How about me?* she nearly said, and almost bit the end of her tongue to stop herself saying it aloud. *What has come over me? It's like I'm dying for him to kiss me or gaze at me the way he did in the isolation block, or take my hand and . . . stop it!*

'Which way now?' asked Harry, and Lola blinked, thankful he hadn't noticed her confusion.

'Over here.' She showed him her mum and Corin's room, pristine in its white and turquoise design; then Sienna's room, all pink and purple and dolphin pictures. At the door to her own room she hesitated. Letting him in here felt very intimate; this was her own space, her private room. 'This is mine.'

'Wow.' Harry raised his eyebrows. 'You like pink.' The walls were a softest rose pink, the carpet pink, and the lampshades, hairbrush, curtains – all varying shades of pink and white.

*It's a little girl's room*, Lola found herself thinking, and she blurted out, 'I'm planning on changing it.' *Wow, am I? Yes, I think I am.* 'It doesn't feel very *me* any more.'

He nodded. 'Right.'

*Why is everything pink and fluffy? It's so – so childish!* Lola felt as though she were seeing the room for the first time. *It doesn't say anything about me, about the person I am. At least – it doesn't seem to fit me any more. Am I changing that much?*

She realized she was just standing there silently, and said hurriedly, 'So, you want to see the next one?'

He replied quickly, 'Yeah, OK.'

With relief, Lola led him out onto the landing again. Her heart was beating much faster than usual, and she felt slightly dizzy. *What's going on with me? Why do I feel as though all this – my house – is too over-the-top? This carpet beneath our feet is about three inches deep. The wall lights are like the ones you'd find in a posh hotel. Even my bed must have cost loads! Now that Harry has seen me here . . . what does he think of me?* 'Uh, these are just guest bedrooms,' she said, waving her hand towards the doors. 'You don't need to see those.' She felt hot and cold all at once. 'And this one's Quinn's room.' She hesitated and then tapped gently on the door. 'Quinn, you there?'

'Yeah. Hang on.' There was the sound of movement, and then Quinn called, 'Come in.'

Lola stuck her head round the door. 'You OK? I've got Harry with me, from the sanctuary. He's come for dinner.'

Quinn's eyebrows climbed into her hair. 'Who?'

Harry edged into the room. 'Hi.'

'Hi.' Quinn looked from Harry to Lola with a slight smile. 'I didn't know you were coming today.'

He shrugged. 'It was kind of last minute.' Then he hesitated. 'Sorry, I'm just – you all look practically identical!'

Lola laughed. 'Yeah, we know.'

'You have a great house,' Harry added.

*Does he hate it?* Lola wondered frantically. She said, 'Mum's suggested we all go for a swim before dinner.'

'Good idea. I need to stay out of her hair for the time being anyway.' Quinn nodded at her. 'I told her about – you know. It was just as we expected, only worse.'

Lola made a face. 'Sorry.'

'I feel better, though,' said Quinn. 'Which proves it's the right decision, doesn't it?'

'I guess so.' Lola hesitated, glancing at Harry. 'Uh – maybe I should explain.'

'No.' He held up his hands. 'You don't have to explain anything. I'm not nosy.'

Quinn laughed. 'You're the opposite to Lola, then!'

Lola shot her an annoyed look. 'I'm not nosy.'

'Not much!' Quinn softened. 'You're not as bad as Sienna, though. Watch out for her, Harry, she'll turn you inside out before you know it.'

He gave her an awkward smile. 'Thanks for the warning.'

# Chapter 14

## it's not what you think

Sienna was floating on her back when they got down to the basement, her silver-clad figure reflected in the pool's ceiling. Harry seemed to have run out of exclamations and simply stared around. 'This is nice,' he said eventually.

Lola bit her lip. 'Yeah, we are lucky.'

He gave her a curious look, and again she had that feeling he was trying to figure her out.

'Harry, there are loads of swim shorts in the end cubicle,' Quinn said, heading towards the end of the pool. 'We keep them for guests. Help yourself to anything that fits.'

'Oh – well, I'm not sure I . . . uh. Maybe I'll just watch.'

'Oh, come on in!' called Sienna from the water. 'It's lovely and warm!' She giggled. 'I promise not to dunk you!'

'Come on.' Lola started off down the side, and reluctantly Harry followed her. As she undressed in the cubicle, Lola automatically reached for her pink swimsuit and then hesitated. No, not the pink one. She was surrounded by pink, wasn't she? Instead, she picked the red gingham one. As she slipped into it, she suddenly wondered what Harry would think. She was almost nervous to come out of the cubicle. Wearing a swimsuit was so – revealing. She felt almost naked! She took a deep breath and unlocked the door.

Seeing Harry in a pair of navy swim shorts took her breath away. He was standing uncertainly by the edge of the pool watching Sienna do some lengths. *Look how fit he is! He's got muscles all over the place!* True, he had pale skin where it hadn't been exposed to the elements, but working outdoors and repairing fences had certainly toned him up. Lola stood and boggled.

'You look like a fish,' said Quinn quietly in her ear, sounding amused.

Lola shut her mouth quickly.

'You like this boy, don't you?' asked Quinn.

'Don't know what you mean,' said Lola. Quinn laughed, tightening the straps on her bikini. 'Are you getting in, Harry?' Lola called.

Harry turned, and she couldn't have wished for a better response from him as he took in her slim figure, tanned an even gold all over. He gulped and turned red. 'Uh, yeah,' he mumbled.

Lola felt a rush of exhilaration. *He's never looked at me like that before!* She couldn't meet his eye, though she felt a big smile spreading over her face. Padding quickly to the deep end, she glanced up to see he was still watching her. 'Best way is to get in quickly,' she called, before executing a perfect racing dive that barely made a splash.

When she surfaced, Sienna swam over to say, 'Great belly-flop, sis.'

'Oh, ha ha. Come on in, Harry, it's really warm.'

'After you,' Quinn said to Harry.

He took a breath. 'Right.' Then he carefully made his way down the steps to the shallow end. The water came up to his chest. He looked awkward.

'Let's play!' cried Sienna, grabbing a shiny beach ball from the side and throwing it towards Harry, who caught it deftly.

Lola was constantly aware of how she looked. As they played catch, she tried to jump out of the water as gracefully as possible; to smooth her hair back from her face so that it didn't make her look like some bedraggled mermaid; to prevent her swimming costume riding up at the back. It was a new feeling, in a way. Sure, she'd wanted boys to notice her in the past, but she'd never felt it was quite so important before. And every time she caught Harry looking at her, she felt warm with pleasure.

'You'll never catch this one!' cried Sienna, throwing the ball high into the air.

Harry, moving forward to reach for the ball, slipped down the slope into the deep end. 'Ha!' cried Sienna, delighted. 'Told you you couldn't reach it!'

But Harry was splashing rather too hard for Lola's liking, and it didn't take her long to realize he was in trouble. He obviously hadn't realized the pool shelved so steeply, but why wasn't he just swimming back?

*He can't swim!*

Before she knew it, Lola had sprung forward to grab Harry's flailing arm and drag him back. Coughing and spluttering, he grasped her gratefully before finding solid ground under his feet and standing up, panting. 'Thanks. Sorry about that.'

'You can't swim, can you?' asked Lola breathlessly.

Harry wiped the water out of his eyes. 'No. So what?' His voice was belligerent.

'I thought everyone could swim,' said Sienna in astonishment. 'Why can't you?'

'Everyone can swim if they have a pool in their basement,' said Harry, looking her straight in the eye.

Sienna bit her lip.

'Didn't you ever have lessons?' asked Lola.

'What for?' Harry shrugged. 'Don't live near the sea, do I?'

'Oh.' Lola didn't know what to say. *Why didn't I ask him beforehand if he could swim? No wonder he wasn't keen to get into the pool!*

'That's OK,' said Quinn. 'We'll teach you.'

Harry looked taken aback. 'Oh, er . . .'

'Yeah!' said Sienna, brightening up. 'I am *such* a good teacher – I taught my friend to swim here too.'

Lola felt a sudden rush of pride. The house might be ostentatious and overwhelming, but her sisters were really nice people, and she was so relieved they had taken to Harry.

Harry looked around at the three gorgeous girls and seemed to decide that it wasn't such a bad idea after all. 'All right.'

'I'll get the floats,' said Sienna immediately.

'Are you sure about this?' Lola asked him in a low voice.

'Sure, why not? You're not going to let me drown, are you?'

She smiled back at him. 'Definitely not.'

The next half hour was filled with giggles and splashing as Harry allowed the three girls to order him around, telling him to kick like *this* or flatten out like *that*. Sienna was in her element, Lola noticed with amusement, her bossy qualities channelled into a positive aim. She was taken aback too by Harry's transformation into a cheerful, joke-playing boy, more like the ones she knew at school. He smiled and laughed readily, 'accidentally' splashing whichever girl got too close and clearly having a brilliant time. But there was no ego there; no showing off. *Samir would have shouted for us to watch him about fifteen times by now*, thought Lola. *And he'd be constantly smoothing his hair back in a TV-advert kind of way. Just as I was a while ago.* She realized that she had practically forgotten about how she looked in all the fun.

'Right,' said Sienna. 'You can do without the floats now. One of us will pull you to the other end of the pool, and you'll have to kick your way back.' She held out her hands. 'Come on.'

'I'm not letting you do it,' Harry told her, laughing. 'You'll let go halfway and make me sink.'

'I would not!'

Harry turned to Lola. 'You do it. You're nicer than she is.'

Sienna blew a loud raspberry at him.

Harry held out his hands to Lola. Smiling, she took

them, and felt her tummy flip at the contact. *Oh dear, this is getting bad now . . . I mustn't let him see I fancy him!*

Carefully, she towed Harry to the other end of the pool, letting him take hold of the side. 'Don't go anywhere,' he said, gripping the tiles for all he was worth.

'I won't,' she said and swallowed, hoping he hadn't noticed the croaky sound to her voice. 'Are you ready?'

'Don't help him!' Sienna called. 'He needs to do it on his own!'

Harry shot Lola a look. 'Your sister likes to order people around, doesn't she?'

Lola grinned. 'Sorry. She's always been like that.'

'I hope it doesn't run in the family,' Harry added. His eyes caught her gaze and held it.

Lola felt her tummy flip again.

'Come on!' shouted Sienna. 'Stop yakking!'

Harry took a breath and launched himself into the water, submerging almost immediately. Breaking the surface of the water, he struggled to regain control before sinking again.

Lola swam forward to help him, and Harry grabbed her hand. 'Tread water,' Lola advised. 'Just pretend you're riding a bicycle.'

Harry raised his eyebrows, though his face was streaming with water. 'I can do that,' he said. Within moments, he had stabilized in the water, though he still gripped Lola's hand. 'Why didn't you say that before?' he asked. 'This is easy.'

Lola laughed. Without thinking, she reached forward to smooth his hair away from his face. Harry blinked as her hand brushed his cheek. 'Thanks,' he said. Where she had touched his face, his cheek reddened slightly.

Lola suddenly found that she was breathing faster. Harry reached for her other hand. 'Don't let me sink,' he said.

'I won't,' she whispered.

Their faces were so close that their legs bumped together as they trod water.

There was a footstep on the stairs above the pool, and then a voice called, 'Lola! Your mum said you were down here—'

Lola swung around to see Samir staring down at them, his face darkening with fury.

♥

'It's not what you think,' Lola said, trying to pull the towelling robe around her more tightly and aware

233

she was dripping water onto her mother's favourite sheepskin rug.

'Isn't it?' asked Samir fiercely.

The two of them had left the pool area and gone up to the sitting room where they couldn't be overheard. Samir was boiling with anger. 'Now I know why you've been so weird with me the last few days. Who is he anyway?'

'It doesn't matter. Samir—'

'It does matter! I suppose he works at your animal place, does he?'

'Well, yes, but—'

'You know what?' Samir glared at her. 'It wouldn't be so bad if you were two-timing me with someone from school. You know? At least I'd feel maybe it was proper competition. But *this* guy!' He stepped back, shaking his head. 'He's a *moose*, Lola!'

Lola flushed. 'He's not a moose! He's really kind . . .'

Samir was nodding. 'I see. I get it. You could at least have had the decency to split up with me before you moved in on someone else.'

'I haven't moved in—'

'Oh, come *on*, Lola! I saw the way you were looking at him! I thought I could trust you. I mean, I'm used to other boys eyeing you up, you're a cute girl, it happens all the time. I came over because Naiha texted me. She said you were playing around with some other guy. I didn't believe her – I thought you were better than that. But now it turns out she was right!'

Lola shivered. The air up here was colder than in the pool room. She pulled the robe more tightly and wished she'd put a towel on her hair. 'Look, Samir, you're cross and I get that . . .'

'I'm more than cross.' Samir's eyes narrowed. 'I've had it. You're *dumped*, Lola. There are other girls lining up for me – any one of them would be more faithful to me than you've been!'

She was overtaken by a sudden fury. 'Like Safi, I suppose?'

'All right, then, if you really want to know, yes, like Safi. She gave me her phone number, but I told her I couldn't go out with her because I already had a girlfriend.' He was red in the face. 'But if I'd known – I'd have called her straight away!'

'Well, now you can!'

'I *will*!'

He turned and walked out.

Lola felt slightly sick. She stood for a moment, taking deep breaths. She'd never seen Samir angry before. He was so easy-going, so laid-back about everything. But he was right, of course. She *did* fancy Harry and there was no getting away from it. In a way, being dumped was the best thing that could have happened, but still Lola felt hurt. She'd never been dumped before and it wasn't nice.

She turned and went back down the stairs to the pool. Sienna was sitting on a bench drying her hair. Quinn was presumably in a cubicle getting changed. 'Where's Harry?' asked Lola.

Sienna made a face. 'Sorry, Lola, he went.'

'Went? What, just now?'

'Yeah. He went out the side door.' Sienna looked apologetic. 'He said he didn't want to cause any trouble and he was going to catch a bus. I tried to get him to stay, I really did.'

'Oh. Oh, right.'

'Did – er . . . what did Samir say?'

'He dumped me.'

'Oh. Sorry, sis.'

'Yeah.' Lola stared at the floor bitterly.

Quinn came out of the cubicle, attired in a powder-blue top and navy jersey trousers. 'Hey, Lola, I'm so sorry. I heard.'

'I guess it was because he saw you with Harry,' Sienna said unhelpfully.

Lola glared at her. 'You think?' She stomped back up the stairs. She'd get changed in her room, in her *pink* room, the one that typified everything about her and her life. The pink room for a pink princess and her perfect Prince Charming.

Only she didn't want Prince Charming any more, did she? She wanted the farm boy instead. *And it's never going to work, because princesses don't go out with farm boys.* She managed to get to her room and close the door before she let the tears slide down her face. *Oh God, how could I let myself fall for someone like Harry?*

# Chapter 15

## what do we do now?

It was Quinn who tapped on Lola's door that night. 'Hey, sweetie. You were so quiet over dinner. You OK?'

Lola sat up in bed and rubbed her eyes. 'No, not really.'

'Tell me about it.' Her sister came round to the side of the bed and gave her a hug. 'Life, huh?'

'I don't know what to do.'

'You like Harry.' It was a statement of fact.

'Yes. But I can't go out with him.'

'Why not?'

Lola gave a small laugh. 'Come on, Quinn. We've got nothing in common.'

'Honey, if you like him – *really* like him – then you can make it work. Honestly.'

'What will everyone say?' Lola asked in a small voice. 'All my friends and . . .'

Quinn paused for a moment and then said, 'I'm not saying it'd be easy. Your friends might be surprised.'

'Surprised? I've been going out with Samir for five months. From him – to Harry? They'll think I've gone mad.'

'Does that matter? They'll come round in the end.'

'I'm not sure.' Lola thought about her friends. 'They'll look down on Harry. And me, if I go out with him.'

'Well, then they're not very nice people,' Quinn told her. 'Harry's lovely.'

Lola looked at her. 'You think so?'

'I do. He's really genuine. He doesn't pretend to be something he's not.' Quinn sighed. 'That's really unusual in a boy.'

'Have you . . . ?' Lola realized she hadn't even asked her sister. 'Have you got a boyfriend?'

'Not at the moment.' Quinn made a rueful face. 'I've had a few bad experiences. Which is why I think you should give it a try with Harry. He's so sweet. Much nicer than Samir.'

'What's wrong with Samir?'

'Too full of himself,' said Quinn promptly. 'Gorgeous, but he knows it.'

'You never said that before.'

Quinn smiled at her affectionately. 'Of course not.

He was your boyfriend. But I never rated him much. He seemed a bit boring to me. It's nice to go out with someone who's interested in stuff that *means* something.' She sighed. 'It's like what I said to you about modelling. It's fun, but it doesn't mean anything. Sometimes it's good to be serious.'

'Harry's serious,' said Lola. She fell silent, remembering how he'd talked to the rescued dog in the strange house. 'And he's got a nice voice.'

'And he's cute,' said Quinn. 'Not in a typical way, but he's got a nice face. Friendly. He listens properly.' She tucked a strand of Lola's hair behind her ear. 'Does he make your stomach go funny when you see him?'

'Yes.'

'Did Samir do that?'

Lola considered. 'Not really. I mean, I would look at him and think *wow, he's gorgeous*, but he didn't make me feel sick.'

Quinn smiled. 'There you go, then.'

'Harry thinks wanting to be a model is stupid.'

'Then he's doubly the right person for you.'

'What did Mum say?' Lola asked. 'When you told her?'

Quinn looked down at her hands. 'Not much. She's gone all quiet on me. Did you see how she avoided talking to me at dinner?'

'Yeah.' It had been a difficult meal, what with Lola having to explain why Harry had gone early and Helena's lips tightening whenever she looked at Quinn. Only Sienna had happily rabbited on – about her new dress for the perfume launch – but Lola had found it hard to care about her sister's clothing.

'She'll come round,' Quinn said hopefully. 'I've been talking to Corin about doing some training at the club.'

'What kind of training?'

'I think I'd like to be a physio,' Quinn said, somewhat surprisingly. 'Or a fitness instructor. Something like that. Corin said I could come in and watch a class or talk to his staff.'

'Wow.'

'I know.' Quinn got up. 'He's a superstar. You OK now?'

'Yeah. Thanks, Quinn.'

'Any time. What are sisters for?'

♥

'You're with the cats today,' Dan said apologetically. 'Sorry, I know they're not your favourite.'

'That's OK.' Lola felt strange being there without Naiha. She wondered what Naiha would be doing that day. More shopping perhaps? 'Er – have you seen Harry this morning?'

'No.' Dan frowned. 'He's not in yet. Not like him.'

Lola felt a clutch of fear at her heart. *Is he avoiding me because of yesterday?* 'Oh. All right.'

She spent the first couple of hours in a kind of stupor. The smell of the cats, so offensive to her nose earlier in the week, hardly bothered her at all now. She listened carefully to Maggie's instructions and then got on with the job, hardly saying a word. Maggie's gaze followed her. 'You OK, Lola?'

'Hm? Oh – yes. Yeah, I'm fine.'

Maggie nodded, and let her get on with it. In some ways, the back-aching work was soothing. Lola knew what she had to do and so she did it without complaint, though she was constantly on the lookout for Harry. *What am I going to say to him?* she wondered. She was single now. Would Harry – her heart thudded loudly – would he want to go out with her? Because one thing was for sure now – she wanted to go out with *him*. There was absolutely no doubt in her mind. He was all she had thought about last night. But after that scene with Samir yesterday in the pool . . . what if Harry thought she was just too much trouble?

Ruth came into the barn, holding a carrier bag.

'Hey, Lola. Um, I brought my jeans, if you . . . if you're still interested . . . '

Lola swung round, relieved to have something else to think about. 'Interested in doing them up? Course I am!'

'Well, thanks.' Ruth handed over the bag, looking shy. 'I put in a couple of tops too – they're really old,' she added hastily. 'Nothing like the lovely clothes you have.'

'That doesn't matter,' Lola told her. 'Besides, don't say old, say vintage.' She grinned.

Ruth smiled back. 'Vintage. Yeah, right.'

'Is there anything in particular that you want me to do? I mean – do you trust me just to be kind of creative with them?'

Ruth nodded. 'I don't mind. Anything to make them feel less like my old – sorry, vintage – clothes. I don't mind being a bit crazy, and nothing matches in my wardrobe anyway.'

'Cool. Have you got a number I can call you on, when they're done?'

'I put it in the bag. Or you could drop them off here when you're passing.' Ruth reddened. 'This is really kind of you, Lola, are you sure you're OK to do it?'

'Yeah, totally. I love messing around with designs.'

Lola smiled. 'I just hope you like what I do with them.'

'I'm sure I will. I've got to get back to the rabbits now – see you later.'

'Bye.'

Maggie was smiling. 'That's thoughtful of you, Lola.'

'It's no problem.' Lola felt pleased that Maggie approved. 'I'll go and put the bag in the office, if that's all right. Back in a minute.'

The office door opened as she got there. 'Oh, Lola,' said Dan. 'I was just coming to find you.' He was smiling. 'I thought you might like to see your dog again? Seeing as it's your last day and all that. She's doing really well – had a good night.' He paused and then said, 'Actually, we wondered if you'd like to name her? She doesn't have a tag and you were the one to find her.'

'Oh!' Lola was speechless. 'I'd love to. Thanks.'

He nodded. 'You've worked hard here this week, Lola. Thanks for your commitment.'

She flushed. 'That's all right. I just need to put this bag in the office before I go.'

He stood aside. 'Of course.'

♥

Lola reached the isolation block and slipped inside. The dog looked up at her entrance and her tail wagged. *She knows me!* She was warmed by the dog's enthusiasm. 'Hello,' she said softly. 'How are you?'

The dog was clearly feeling a lot better. Her eyes were bright and her nose wet. She was still as thin as ever, though, and Lola felt her heart constrict as she lifted the little animal out of the cage and felt her ribs through the skin. 'We need to feed you up,' she said. The dog licked her hand. 'And what am I going to call you?' Lola thought of all the names she had chosen for the imaginary Pomeranian. Cookie, Princess, Sweetie, Fifi . . . none of them was right for this dog! 'You need a proper name,' Lola told her. 'Not a silly one.'

The door opened. 'She's looking so much better,' said Lola, without glancing up. 'And she likes me!'

'Of course she does,' came Harry's voice. 'Who wouldn't?'

Lola felt dizzy for a moment. *I'm not ready! I haven't decided what to say!* Swallowing, she looked up at him. 'Hi.'

He met her gaze. 'Hi.'

*Something's changed*, she thought hazily. *He's looking at me differently.* 'Uh . . . everything OK?'

'No, not really.'

*Oh God. He's talking about what happened yesterday.*
'Look, I'm really sorry—'

'I got locked out of my house last night,' he interrupted.

'What?'

He sighed and sat down on the floor next to her. 'My brother was in one of his moods. I forgot he'd asked me to get bread from the shop on my way home. When I was late coming back, he bolted the front door.'

Lola stared. 'What did you do?'

'Banged on the door,' said Harry with a shrug. 'For about half an hour until my neighbour threatened to call the police.'

'Oh my God. Did he let you in?'

'No.' Harry yawned. 'He said he wouldn't unbolt the door till the morning.'

'What about your parents?'

'Passed out in some kind of drunken coma, I think. They didn't care.' He stroked the dog. 'In the end I climbed up the drainpipe at the back of the house and broke my own bedroom window so I could get in.'

'You broke the window?' Lola gasped. 'What with?'

'A brick.' Harry rubbed his knuckles and pulled

a face. 'Windows are harder than you think, actually.'

'Didn't you get cut?'

'I wrapped my T-shirt round my hand first.' He gave her a small smile. 'I did get bruised, though.'

She reached out. 'Let me see.'

Even in the dim light she could see the purple bruises swelling on his hand. She ran her thumb over them lightly. 'You poor thing. I'm so sorry.' Then without even thinking, she lifted his hand to her mouth and kissed it. It felt like the most natural thing in the world.

Harry's breath caught in his throat and Lola felt the air around them fizz with heat. 'Lola . . .' he said in a whisper.

'Yes?' she breathed, not daring to look at him. The moment felt balanced on a knife edge – one false move could ruin everything. So Lola kept perfectly still, and by some kind of telepathy the dog in her lap also froze in position, ears twitching at the unseen electricity.

Harry took her hand in his, and lifted it in turn to his mouth. Lola closed her eyes as he kissed it, the touch sending tingling fireworks through her whole arm. Then before she knew it, his lips were on hers and his hands were in her hair, and everything was melting . . .

*I've never felt anything like this* . . . was the last

thought that went through her head before the world went multicoloured.

It may have been a minute, it may have been an hour – time ceased to have meaning, and the only reason they broke apart was because the little dog shifted position and tried to lick Lola's ear. 'Ew! What was – oh, it was the dog.'

Harry laughed, and the sound spread warmth through Lola like sunshine. 'Maybe she thought we were taking too long.'

Lola looked shyly at him. 'I didn't think it was long enough.'

'Me neither. Put the dog back so we can do it again.'

Stifling a laugh, Lola lifted the dog back into the pen, stroking her gently. 'You have a rest,' she told the animal. 'Be with you in a minute.'

The second kiss was even better than the first, if such a thing were possible. But when they broke apart again, Harry took her face in his hands and said seriously, 'What do we do now?'

Lola's head was still fuzzy, but she knew what he meant. 'I – well, what do *you* want?' *Please say you want to go out with me!*

He looked at her intently, studying her face. 'Lola, I really like you. I mean – a lot. I – you – of all the girls I've met, you're the only one who . . . well.' He shrugged and his hands dropped away. 'I thought when we met that you were just an airhead.'

'Hey!'

'All that stuff about modelling and your hair and your nails.' He grinned. 'Proper boring, you were. But then . . . I got to know you a bit more, and you're not really like that at all.'

'I'm not?'

'You're funny and you're kind, and you care about other things and other people and not just yourself.'

She blushed. 'I didn't—'

'And of course you're pretty,' he went on, as though he'd only just thought of it, 'but lots of girls are pretty.'

Lola bridled. 'Not *all* girls,' she said huffily.

Harry laughed again. 'You want me to say it? All right – you're gorgeous. You really are. You and your sisters – you're all stunning, amazing-looking. Your hair . . .' He reached out to touch it. 'It's like gold. But I don't care about your hair. I don't care about your nails or your nose, or – or whatever. I like the bit in *here* . . .' His finger touched her gently at the base of her neck. 'In here is who you really are.'

'You can't know who I really am,' breathed Lola, shaken. 'You've only known me four days.'

'Five,' he said, 'counting today.' And then he kissed her again.

*This is it,* thought Lola. *This is the moment. He's going to ask me out. We're going to be a couple – boyfriend and girlfriend . . .* An image swam before her closed eyes: the two of them holding hands, laughing, talking to Lola's other friends . . . The same small worry began to nibble away at her again. What would *they* say? Her family had been kind to Harry, but then they were pleased if Lola was happy. Her friends – they were different. Lola and Samir had been the golden couple of their year. What would everyone say if Lola started going out with Harry right after being dumped by the most popular boy in school? And what would they say about Harry himself? When Lola had raised this worry with Quinn, her sister had said they weren't good friends if they didn't accept Harry, but it wasn't that simple, was it?

This time, she was the first to pull away. Harry looked at her, his cheeks still flushed, a frown creasing his forehead. 'What's wrong?'

Lola stared at the floor. 'I don't – I'm just not sure . . .' She stopped, biting her lip.

'What do you mean?' Harry was confused. 'Not sure about what?'

'Not sure about . . . us.' It was so painful to say it!

*I can't believe I'm doing this*, Lola's brain raced. *I want to be with him so much! But – what about the other part of my life? The people I hang out with* . . . She just knew they wouldn't be so accepting of Harry. There would be jeers, laughter. Maybe some of her friends wouldn't want to know her any more. Harry wasn't just another boy from school – he was different. He'd never fit in. How could she cope with that? *I've changed . . . but am I brave enough to change this much?*

He reached for her. 'Don't say it.'

Suddenly, the words came tumbling out. 'Harry, I really like you. That was – wow. I don't know how to describe it. I – you – you're not what I expected. I didn't expect to like you. And now, I can't stop thinking about you.'

'Me too.'

'But it's not that simple. We're different.' Lola screwed up her eyes. 'You and me – it can't work.'

'Why not?' Harry's expression was darkening.

'We're just – well, look at us.'

'Are you saying I'm not good enough for you?' His voice was quiet, but there was something dangerous in it.

'No, of course not . . .'

'Would you rather go back to that pretty boyfriend?'

'Samir? No, we split up, I don't—'

'Because that's what it sounds like. You're saying you should only go out with boys like him. I'm *beneath* you, is that right?'

'No!' Tears sprang to her eyes. 'That's not it at all!'

'Isn't it?' He leaned towards her, staring hard. 'Look me in the eye and tell me it's not because you look down on me and my family.'

Her gaze wobbled. 'I don't even know your family,' she said miserably, looking away.

'No,' he agreed. 'You don't.' And the anger in his voice made her flinch.

'I'm sorry. I didn't mean . . .'

'I know. It's just how you are. You don't have to apologize. It's what you're used to – things being easy for you.' He sighed. 'I know we're different. But I don't care about things like that. I think that if you . . .' he swallowed, 'you care about someone, then you can work all that other stuff out. I thought you'd feel the same way.'

Lola felt the tears run down her face, but she didn't know how to answer. Because he was right, wasn't he? She wasn't ready to risk the ridicule of her friends – look how Naiha had reacted! What if everyone else reacted the same way? She would have no friends – no one to hang out with at school. 'I thought I did . . .'

she said, the sobs rising in her throat. 'I honestly thought ... but it's so hard.'

Harry put his hand on his chest, as though something hurt him. 'Sorry, Lola. I have to go. Dogs need walking.'

'No, please ... please, it's my last day ...'

Through a haze of tears she watched him leave.

# Chapter 16

## why can't you just be happy with what you've got?

'Thanks for all your hard work, Lola.' Dan shook her hand. Ruth and Maggie had already said their goodbyes, but Lola hadn't had a chance to speak to Harry since that morning. He'd passed her on his way to walking the dogs, but had made no attempt to talk to her, and Lola felt as though her heart were being squeezed into a pulp.

'We've really enjoyed having you here this week,' Dan said. Lola was thankful he hadn't asked her how she was, since it must be obvious she'd been crying. He smiled. 'Any time you want a job here, just let me know.'

She nodded miserably, hardly hearing him.

'And as for the dog you rescued, we'll take good care of her and find her a nice new home.'

'Oh. Yes – yes, a really nice one.' Lola felt a sudden

pang at the idea of her little dog going to live with strangers.

Dan tilted his head to one side. 'Have you thought about adopting her yourself? Does your family like dogs?'

'Um – we don't have any pets . . . but I could ask.' It was a lovely idea. Maybe she could get her mother on side?

'Have you decided what to call her?'

'Harriet.' It was as close to 'Harry' as she could get in a girl's name. Dan raised his eyebrows, so Lola felt she had to explain. 'Because Harry was really the one who rescued her; I just went along with it. He's the real reason she's safe – he stood up to that man and everything.'

Dan smiled. 'I bet he's made up about it.'

'I – I haven't told him. He – er – I haven't had a chance to speak to him since I decided.' Impulsively, she said, 'Will you tell him? And – and can you give him this?' She held out a piece of paper. 'I've written him a note, because I haven't seen him since – since earlier.' The words rushed out in embarrassment.

Dan took the piece of paper. 'Of course. Are you sure you don't want to go find him yourself?'

'No. No, that's all right.' *Except it isn't. It isn't all right at all, everything's all wrong . . .*

'OK. Well, thanks again, and I'll be sure to give your school a great report on you.'

She smiled, although she couldn't have cared less. Back to school next week – back to things being the way they were before . . . before she met Harry and he changed her life.

She smiled again, though it was an effort, and, grasping her bag, closed the office door behind her for the last time.

♥

'I bet you're glad it's all over,' Sienna commented at dinner. 'No more clearing up poo!'

Lola poked at her mashed potato. 'Oh, it was all right.'

'That's not what you said at the beginning of the week. Remember you wanted to get transferred to something else?' Sienna snorted. 'Can't say I blame you.'

'Maybe Lola found it wasn't so bad after all,' suggested Quinn gently.

'Yeah, because of *Harry* . . .' Sienna's voice took on a teasing tone. 'When's he coming round again then? He was a laugh.'

'He's not.' Lola put down her fork. 'Look, I don't really want to talk about this, OK?'

Her mother glanced at her in concern. 'You not hungry, Lola?'

'No.'

'I expect you're just tired,' said Helena comfortingly. 'It's been a long, hard week for you.' She brightened up. 'How about tomorrow we go into town and have a spa day?'

'Ooh, *yes*,' said Sienna delightedly. 'Can I have the aromatherapy facial again? It was so lush!'

Lola tried to smile, but somehow the thought of a spa day didn't excite her in the way it used to. *Aromatherapy facial?* she thought despairingly. *Who cares? How am I going to persuade my parents to let me have a dog, so that Harriet doesn't go to someone else?*

'I've got to get back to London,' said Quinn regretfully. Her gaze met her mother's. 'Got a few things to sort out.'

Helena made a non-committal noise. 'You should go to that man I suggested too,' she added. 'He could really help.'

'Mum, I don't need a life coach. Or therapy.'

'Helena, let's see how she gets on when she comes back here,' Corin suggested. 'Maybe a change of direction is all she needs.'

'Speaking of directions,' said Quinn, 'can you look

at my sat nav? It keeps showing the wrong time and I can't remember how to change it.'

Corin nodded. 'Is that Mini still running OK?'

'It's gorgeous.'

'Good. I was thinking of getting a new car.'

'Is there something wrong with the Audi?' asked Helena.

'No, I just feel like a change.'

'Well, you can't have my Mini,' said Quinn, laughing. 'Which car are you looking at? There's an amazing new Porsche . . .'

Corin waved away the suggestion. 'No, no, I know the one you're talking about. No, I was wondering about an MG.'

Quinn frowned. 'They're kind of small. Don't you pick up Sienna and Lola from school sometimes?'

'Oh, I'd keep the Audi for that,' said Corin. 'No, the MG would be an extra.'

Quinn nodded. 'I see. I know a designer who drives an MG F. He says it's a dream.'

'I want a Beetle,' announced Sienna. 'In blue.'

'You can't drive.' Quinn grinned at her.

'I know that.' Sienna was affronted. 'Just saying – my seventeenth birthday is only five years away.'

'You'll have changed your mind before then!'

'I'd have to move that old Golf out of the garage,'

went on Corin, 'to make room. In fact, we could even get rid of the Golf.'

'Oh, but it's the perfect car for Lola and Sienna to practise on, when they're old enough to drive,' objected Helena. 'We've got enough room round by the greenhouse, you could put it there.'

'I want a Beetle,' said Sienna obstinately. 'I don't like the Golf; it smells.'

'Oh, for God's sake!' cried Lola. Everyone turned to look at her. 'It's a *car*, isn't it? It works! What's the fuss about? Why can't you just be happy with what you've got?'

Her family turned to look at her, shock in their faces. 'I think you might be over-reacting just a little, Lola,' said Corin.

'What's wrong with wanting a nice car?' Sienna challenged.

'Nothing,' said Lola, 'but we've *got* cars already – several of them!'

'Lola, darling,' said her mother in a reasonable tone, 'what's brought this on?'

'I just think,' Lola said fiercely, 'that we have too much *stuff*, that's all. Stuff we don't even need. All this money – can't we spend it on things that *matter*?'

She saw her parents exchange glances. 'Like what?' asked Corin.

'I don't know! But there are loads of people out there who need help – loads of projects that need money. How much do we actually give to charity?'

'More than you think,' said Corin sharply.

'Hang on a minute,' said Sienna, her eyes narrowing. 'This is to do with that scruffy animal sanctuary, isn't it? You're trying to make us feel bad because you've spent a week grubbing around in the dirt while we went shopping.'

'Some people don't get to go shopping,' Lola snapped.

Sienna rolled her eyes. 'Oh, puh-*lease*. Lighten up, Lola. Since you started working there, you've got all serious. I don't like the new Lola; she's boring!'

'She's not boring, she's growing up,' said Quinn quietly. Her eyes met Lola's. 'I do like the new Lola, actually.'

Lola felt a tiny flicker of warmth. 'Thanks, Quinn.'

'Let me guess,' Sienna said, rolling her eyes. 'You think we should give loads of money to the people at the animal sanctuary, right?'

'I never said that,' replied Lola defensively. 'But they do spend hours every week working for pennies because they really *care* about animals. If they didn't, those animals would all have to be put down. And their buildings are all falling apart and they can't even

260

afford heating for the office.'

'That's not *your* problem,' Sienna pointed out. 'They should get money from the Government or something.'

'Well, they don't.'

'I don't see why we couldn't make a donation to the sanctuary.' Corin looked at his wife. 'It would be a kind of thank you for taking Lola on at such short notice.'

'They don't need thanks, they need funding!' exclaimed Lola. 'Just to help them keep going. Do you know how much it costs to run the place? There's a chart on the wall of the office. It takes three quarters of a million pounds a year!'

Helena laughed. 'We don't have quite that much to throw away, darling.'

'It wouldn't be throwing it away – oh, never mind!' Lola pushed back her chair. 'I'm going to my room. And that's another thing. I don't want it pink any more, I'm going to redesign.'

'What's wrong with pink?' asked Sienna sarcastically. 'It's just a room, after all. You could give the design money to the *sanctuary* instead!'

'Sienna . . .' said her mother in a warning voice.

Lola ignored them all as she sprinted up the stairs. Confused thoughts swam around her head. What *did* she want exactly? *And who am I now?*

When she reached her room, her eyes fell on the bag of clothes from Ruth. *That's where I'll start*, she told herself. *My room can wait. These are more important.*

♥

Returning to school on Monday felt strange to Lola. She'd got so used to throwing on jeans and a thick jumper that it was odd to be back in uniform and wondering what inventive things to do with her hairstyle. Normally she'd have met Naiha at the school gates, but Naiha hadn't been in touch since storming out of the sanctuary on Thursday, and Lola hadn't tried to text her. The way Naiha had behaved – including telling Samir that Lola was cheating on him! – she didn't think she wanted to be friends ever again.

Tasha and Alisha had been in touch over the weekend. It was clear that Naiha had told them her version of events and they thought she'd been right to walk out of her work experience. Lola had tried to explain, but her friends obviously thought the row would blow over and she and Naiha would be friends again soon. Of more interest to them was the fact that she and Samir were no longer an item. Tasha in particular asked a lot of questions, mainly about how Lola would feel if Samir went out with one of her friends. Lola sighed. 'You're welcome to him,' she said, before refusing their invitation to meet up on Sunday for shopping. 'I've got stuff to do,' she said vaguely, thinking of Ruth's clothes and how much she was enjoying doing them up.

It was nice to see the other people in her form, and to hear more about their experiences of the previous week, but Lola felt somehow disconnected from it all. *I don't wish I was still at the sanctuary*, she told herself. *I don't wish I was still clearing up cat poo. So why can't I just enjoy being back in my real life?* Samir sat on the other side of the classroom and laughed with his friends. He didn't look at her once, and she didn't care.

*Harry.* That was why she couldn't click back into her old life, she knew. Since that Friday evening, she had barely thought about anything else. Over and over again, she'd replayed the scene in the isolation shed, his arms around her, the amazing kisses. *Was I wrong?* she wondered. *Should I have said yes, let's be an item and stuff what everyone else thinks? Have I made the biggest mistake ever?*

It was so confusing. Lola felt as though she were in some way at a crossroads in her life. Everything up to now had been given to her. She'd been brought up to be polite and well-groomed, but she couldn't remember anyone ever suggesting she should *care* about stuff outside her own life experience. And now she found herself thinking of Ruth's face as she stared worriedly at the poorly rabbit; of Maggie's warmth and her affection for the cats she looked after; of Graham, the blind boy who came to stroke the animals because it made him happy. And of Harry, of course – the boy who bunked off school so that he could go and mend fences, train dogs, be useful. The boy who had found a place in life and was happy there.

Because Harry *was* happy there, wasn't he? He obviously didn't have much fun at home. He had parents who drank and didn't care about him; he had an older brother who locked him out of the house. He'd been thrown out of school because he got into fights. But at the sanctuary, he was happy. There, he was appreciated. People asked him for help and he gave it. He loved the dogs, especially the fierce ones. And Dan said he'd turned his life around; that he was finally making something of himself. That was worth a lot, wasn't it? Didn't it show that he was a decent person, determined to find his own path in the world?

Where did she want her path in life to take her? *I thought I knew . . . but I'm not sure any more . . .*

'Lola?'

Lola blinked. The whole class was staring at her. 'Huh? What?'

Her maths teacher wore a sarcastic expression. 'Were you planning to join us today, Lola, or were you going to spend the whole lesson gazing out of the window? Some things never change.'

Naiha, sitting nearby, sniggered. She whispered to the girl sitting next to her and they both laughed.

*I have changed*, Lola thought rebelliously. *I have – I'm not the same person I was a week ago.* But she didn't dare say it out loud. Alisha gave her a sympathetic smile before raising her hand to answer Lola's question. 'It's all right,' she whispered a few minutes later. 'I could guess what you were thinking about.'

Lola looked up, alert.

Alisha nodded. 'It's written all over your face. You were thinking about Samir, right? And how you can get him back?'

'No!' The word came out louder than she had intended, and the teacher looked over, annoyed. Lola didn't dare say more but she shook her head vehemently. No, no, no – she had *not* been thinking about Samir! But the expression on her face must have shown she'd been thinking of someone she cared about.

*Well, it doesn't matter anyway*, Lola thought as she picked up her pen and tried to concentrate. *It doesn't matter if I was thinking about Harry, since I'll never see him again.*

A tear dripped onto her book and blotted the quadratic equation she'd just written.

# Chapter 17

## harriet

'There you are,' said Helena, tearing off the cheque. It was made out to the Parchester Animal Sanctuary, and it was for a lot of money.

'Thanks, Mum.'

Lola's mother folded away her cheque book. 'No problem, darling. You're right, we do need to think about helping others more. I've asked Cleo to give some launch party tickets to a local women's shelter. They can come along and have goodie bags if they like.'

Lola knew her mum meant well, though she wondered what the women from the shelter would think of the glitzy bash. 'That's nice, Mum.'

Helena dropped a kiss on her head. 'You're so serious these days, sweetie. Ever since you worked at that place. And your English teacher said you've written an amazing essay about it. Bound to be an

A-star she said. An A-star – for my Lola! I'm so proud of you!'

'Yeah.' Lola found it hard to be pleased about that, even though it would be the first time she'd been given such a high grade. She hadn't written the essay for the marks; she'd written it because, two weeks on, the sanctuary was still very much on her mind. And today was the day she was going back. Her stomach was flipping around so much, she hadn't been able to eat any breakfast.

Corin breezed into the sitting room. 'You ready, Lola?'

She took a breath. 'Yes.'

'Now, you said we won't be taking the dog away today, is that right?'

'No, Dan has to do all the paperwork.' Lola was nervous but excited. Who'd have thought she'd be able to persuade her parents to let her adopt Harriet? It had taken two weeks of begging because both her mother and stepdad had been reluctant. 'Have you really thought about this?' Corin had asked. 'A dog isn't something you can put in a drawer when you've finished playing with it.'

Lola had been irritated. 'I know that. I'll look after her, I promise. I know what she'll need, and

I'm not going to get bored or forget my respon-
sibilities.'

Corin had raised his eyebrows and glanced at his
wife. After that, they had been more positive about
the idea.

Lola felt sick with nerves as she got into Corin's car.
Would Harry be there? He hadn't called. She supposed
she shouldn't have expected him to. She hoped he had
at least read her note, giving him her phone number
and saying she was so sorry about everything. Her
fingers wrapped themselves around the handles of
the carrier bag containing Ruth's finished clothes.
Lola had spent a lot of time on them, adding darts,
knotted ribbons, and neat stitches in patterns. She
was pleased with the results and had really enjoyed
the work. But the butterflies in her stomach were
flapping so hard that she could barely think about
anything but Harry.

Corin suddenly exclaimed, 'Oh, I forgot to mention.
Did you ask the skating girl, Tania Dunn, if she'd like
to be in the photoshoot for the new banners for the
club?'

'Yes! Yes, I did. Oh – she gave me her phone number
and everything! Sorry, I'd forgotten all about it.'

Corin grinned. 'Don't apologize. Her mum
rang yesterday to find out if we still wanted her.

Good work, Lola, she's a great role model for young people. I'd be delighted to have her advertising the club.'

Lola felt pleased. 'I thought she'd look good in a ballet pose or yoga or something. You know, maybe with blue chiffon drapes behind in a kind of marquee look?'

Corin shot her a sideways glance. 'That sounds good. To be honest, I'm not one hundred per cent happy with the designs the new company is coming up with. I'm not convinced they've quite got the right angle yet.' He hesitated. 'I know you said you'd like to be involved – to come and give an opinion. Do you still want to?'

'Oh, yes!' Lola was surprised and thrilled. 'That would be brilliant – are you sure?'

'It won't hurt for you to come in and see what you think,' said Corin. 'You've got a good eye for that kind of thing. And this new Lola . . . I like her.' He smiled. 'It feels like you've grown up all of a sudden. I guess I've always seen you and Sienna as the babies of the family. But you're growing up, and it's time I gave you more of a chance.'

Lola blushed with pleasure. 'Thanks, Corin. I do feel kind of different.'

Then they turned in to the driveway of the sanctuary

and the blush faded from her cheeks. She gripped the bag more tightly.

'Here we are,' said Corin. 'Can you get the gates for me?'

There was no one in sight as Lola opened the gates and then closed them again behind Corin's car. She couldn't help looking around.

'Is this the office?' asked Corin.

'Yes.' Lola suddenly remembered how the office had appeared to her on her first day. Now, the battered little shed seemed quite different to her eyes. She knocked on the door.

'Come in!'

Dan was sitting behind his desk and grinned as the two of them came in. 'Lola! Great to see you. How is everything?'

'Good, thanks.'

'You must be Mr Kellerman.' Dan got up to shake Corin's hand. 'Nice to meet you.' He looked at Lola again. 'Shall we go and see Harriet before we do the paperwork?'

'Oh, yes please!'

Dan smiled at her. 'She's looking quite different from the last time you saw her.'

Harriet was no longer being kept in the isolation shed. Instead, Dan led them round to the dog yard.

Lola's heart thumped as they walked into the area Harry loved best. There was no sign of him, but a volley of barking broke out as they approached.

Lola spotted Harriet immediately. She was standing at the front of the pen, her tail wagging hard, though she didn't make a sound. 'She remembers you,' said Dan with a smile.

Lola bent down. 'Hello, Harriet. You look amazing!' Harriet had filled out and no longer looked like the skinny little thing she had been two weeks ago. She still had a cast on her leg, but she was moving around a lot more easily. She snuffled quietly into Lola's hand, licking her fingers. 'I can't believe how good she looks.' Lola looked up at Dan. She felt an enormous wave of happiness. 'It's like she's a different dog.'

Corin was wearing a surprised expression. 'This is Harriet? She doesn't look anything like I imagined. I thought you wanted a toy dog, Lola, one of those Pom-Pom dogs or something.'

'That was before I met Harriet.' Lola turned back to the little mongrel in the cage. 'You're coming home with me, Harriet. Not today – but very soon. I can't wait to show you the bed we've got for you!'

'I'm glad she's going home with you,' said Dan. 'You're the one who rescued her, after all.'

'Me and Harry,' Lola corrected him. 'Is he – is he here?'

'Well, not today, he isn't. There's been a—'

'Lola!' Ruth came running over. 'How are you?'

'I'm fine, thanks, Ruth, how are you?'

Ruth ran a hand through her dandelion-clock hair. 'I'm good. Have you got them?'

Lola held out the bag. She had a momentary qualm. 'Here you go. I hope you like them.'

Ruth pulled the clothes out of the bag, uttering little squeaks of excitement. 'These look amazing! Look at this patch here – and the stitching down the seams – and this sparkly bit. Lola, you're so clever!' She frowned. 'But you weren't supposed to use anything expensive. These sparkly bits – they must have cost—'

'They didn't,' Lola interrupted. 'Honestly. I had some in my sewing basket anyway, and the rest I got off an old top of mine.'

'Well, if you're sure . . . I can't believe it! My clothes don't look anything like they used to!'

Lola smiled. 'I really enjoyed doing it all. And you like it – what I've done?'

Ruth beamed. 'I do. They're brilliant. I don't suppose . . . ' She hesitated. 'My sister runs a youth centre in Parchester. Would you come and do a workshop? Show the kids how to do this kind of thing? My sister's always looking for ways to keep them interested.'

'Oh!' Lola was taken aback. 'Well, I guess so . . . do you really think they'd want to?'

Ruth nodded. 'I'm positive. There are loads of girls there, and of course they all want new clothes and things, but their parents can't always afford them.'

Lola felt uncomfortable. Her parents had always been able to buy her whatever was in fashion. But maybe this was her chance to 'give something back'? To do something that meant something, like Quinn said. She made up her mind. 'I'd love to. Give your sister my phone number and tell her to ring me.'

'I will.' Ruth gave her a sudden hug. 'Thanks so much. I can't wait to try these on!' She dashed off.

Corin was looking impressed, but before he could say anything, Dan broke in with, 'Shall we go and do the forms, then? And Lola, you can ask any questions you have about keeping a dog.'

They headed back to the office, Lola waving goodbye to Harriet, whose tail drooped as she walked away. Lola felt bad for leaving her. *But it's only for a few more days*, she told herself.

'I can see many of your buildings could do with some repair work,' commented Corin.

Dan nodded. 'We do our best, but there's always a lot to do.'

'Lola's been telling us how much your sanctuary needs each year to run. Vets' bills and food and everything.' Corin glanced across at her. 'She's been quite changed by this experience.'

Lola felt embarrassed.

Dan smiled. 'Many people are changed by working here. Animals are very different to people.'

'We brought a cheque,' said Lola, pulling it out of her pocket and holding it out. 'It's – er – for anything you need, really.'

'That's very kind . . .' said Dan, before he looked at it. Then his eyes flicked up to hers, shocked.

'I'm sorry it's not more,' Lola felt compelled to say.

'This is a lot of money, Lola,' Dan said, and his voice was suddenly hoarse. 'Are you sure?'

'She's sure,' said Corin. 'We all are. We talked about it at home.'

'Well,' said Dan, and swallowed. 'Well. That's very kind. Thank you.' He folded the cheque carefully and put it in his shirt pocket. 'I don't know what to say. Thank you. It will be put to very good use.'

'I'm sure it will,' replied Corin.

Once inside the office, Dan almost seemed to have forgotten why they were there. He was clearly still shaken by the gift. 'Sorry, um . . . where were we? Paperwork. Right. Adoption papers.'

Corin sat in the chair opposite. 'You must have a lot of people come to adopt animals.'

'Oh, a fair amount. It varies from week to week.' Dan bent down to look in a filing cabinet. 'Hang on, here we go . . .'

'Lola told us about how she rescued the dog,' Corin went on. 'I have to say, we weren't impressed to hear she'd been breaking into a house, but we're glad it all ended well.'

Dan opened his mouth and then shut it again. He glanced at Lola. 'Mm.'

Lola frowned. 'What is it?'

'It didn't end quite so well as we'd hoped,' said Dan slowly. 'I was going to tell you earlier . . .'

'Tell me what?'

'It's about Harry.'

Fear gripped her. 'Tell me!'

'That man who was squatting in the house – the one who had the dog.'

'Yes?'

'Well, it seems the police tried to move him on. Someone had reported that he was living there.'

Lola caught her breath. 'Harry?'

'No – no, it wasn't Harry. But the man thought

it was.' He hesitated again. 'He ambushed Harry. Yesterday evening. That's why he's not here. Harry's in hospital.'

♥

Lola's heart felt as though it were jumping around inside her ribs as she pushed open the double doors of the hospital ward. She had wanted to leave Corin at the main entrance, but he insisted on coming with her up to the ward. 'There's nothing to worry about,' he kept saying. 'Dan said it was a broken wrist and concussion, and some bruises. It's not as serious as it might have been.'

Lola was barely listening. 'I know, I know. But I feel like it's all my fault.'

'How could it be? It's just one of those things.' Corin sounded anxious. 'Thank goodness they've caught the man who did it. You might have to talk to the police, I suppose, Lola. If they want to know about when you met him.'

'Whatever.' She didn't care about that; she just wanted to see Harry. Something inside her hurt terribly. He was injured and she hadn't known! It was so important that she got to see him!

They went to the ward Dan had described, and

Corin asked at the reception desk. 'Oh yes,' said the nurse. 'He's in bay seventeen. Are you family?'

'Just friends,' said Corin.

The nurse smiled. 'I'm glad he's got visitors. He's a nice lad. Come on, I'll take you round.'

'I'll wait here,' Corin said, 'if you'd prefer?'

Lola nodded. 'Is that OK? I'd rather see him . . . on my own.'

'That's fine. I brought my iPad, take your time.'

Lola followed the nurse round the corner and into a bay of six beds. Instantly, she spotted Harry. He was sitting up in bed, his face pale against the white sheets. One arm was in plaster up to the elbow, and a large black and purple bruise was spreading over one cheekbone. He turned and saw her, and if she had any doubt about how he felt about her it disappeared in the way his face lit up.

'Hey,' he said, his eyes shining. 'It's you.'

She felt an absurd desire to cry. His face! His lovely face – and those eyes. *I missed him so much! Even more than I thought . . .*

'I'll be at the desk if you need anything,' said the nurse, tactfully withdrawing.

Lola glanced at the other beds. Two were occupied, but one of the men was asleep whilst the other was deep into a book. Hesitantly, she made her way over to Harry, feeling trembly. There was a chair by the bed, so she perched on the edge. 'How – how are you?'

'I'll live,' he said, grinning.

Lola felt her eyes brimming with tears. She reached in her bag for a tissue, her heart sinking as she realized she hadn't got any.

'Hey, what's the matter?' asked Harry, concerned. Lola tried to wipe the tears away on her sleeve. His expression changed. 'Do I look that bad?'

She gave a shaky laugh. 'Of course not. You look fine.'

'You're a bad liar. I've got a massive shiner . . .' He touched the bruise gingerly and winced. 'But it'll be all right. My eye isn't about to fall out or anything.'

'Dan said you had concussion.'

'Yeah, not badly, though. I mean, I passed out for a few minutes and then it's all a bit of a blur until I woke up here.'

'Did he – did he hit you?' Lola asked, and swallowed. 'The man, the homeless man.'

'What, on the head?' asked Harry. 'No, I did that bit myself. Fell over and hit it on a wall. Stupid.'

'But Dan said . . .'

'Oh, yeah – yeah, he *hit* me. The guy from the house. He was really mad; said we'd taken away everything he had – the dog and the house and stuff. I could see he wasn't going to let me speak. He was gearing up for a fight.' He grimaced. 'He's stronger than he looks – faster too.'

Lola glanced at the plaster on his arm. 'Was that . . . ?'

'Yeah. Not nice.' Harry didn't seem inclined to elaborate.

'What happened? I mean . . . '

Harry understood. 'He'd been waiting for me, in that park area, you know where we take the dogs every day? There wasn't anyone else about. It was the perfect ambush. He starts yelling at me, and then just lays into me.' He gave a short laugh. 'It was the dogs in the end that saved me. You remember Groucho? The Rottweiler? Somehow he got his muzzle off, grabbed the bloke's arm and bit him so hard, the man ran off. The police got him an hour later, when he turned up in Casualty demanding to be stitched up. Luckily they're not blaming Groucho for the bite; they say the man brought it on himself. Just as well, otherwise Groucho could have been put down.'

'Oh, Harry . . .' Lola felt the tears start up again and tried to blink them back.

'I've had worse,' said Harry.

'Really?'

'Well, all right, no one's ever broken my wrist before. But I wouldn't still be in hospital if I hadn't bashed my head. Thing is, I feel fine now, but they won't let me go home till tomorrow.' He looked at her. 'Thanks for coming. Were you at the sanctuary then?'

'Yes, my parents have agreed I can adopt Harriet, hadn't you heard?'

He gave a half-hearted shrug. 'Sort of. Ruth told me, but it was in with trying to find out why I wasn't in touch with you. She said something about a conversation she had with you – about me. She kept going on about barriers. I told her it was none of her business.'

Lola dropped her gaze. 'Oh.' There was a pause. *Now*, her mind said, *now's the time to tell him how you feel*. But she chickened out. 'Where's your family? Haven't your parents come?'

'Yeah, my mum came as soon as she heard. But she's no use, just got really upset and then had to go home and lie down. And Dad came for about ten minutes to make sure I wasn't dead. Then he went back to the pub. My brother didn't bother to come; no great loss. So . . . it's nice to see you.'

'It's nice to see you too,' she said, meeting his gaze.

'Lola—'

'Listen,' she interrupted, 'I've got to talk to you. I

mean, I've got to tell you . . .' She took a breath. 'I'm so sorry about before. I wasn't fair. I – I was scared.'

'I know.' His voice was gruff. 'It's OK, you don't have to explain.'

'No, it's not OK. You made me see things in a different way. You and the sanctuary. You were right when you said that there was more to me than hairstyles and nail varnish. I just didn't know it myself until you said it.' He was looking down at the sheets, his face reddening. 'All my life I've had money and things,' she went on rapidly, hoping her courage wouldn't desert her. 'It's not that I've been really spoilt, it's more that I've never thought about it. I haven't appreciated it because I haven't ever had to live without stuff. And my friends too – they've always been . . .' She gulped. 'They've been like me. And so I grew up thinking that was normal, that it didn't matter how other people lived or what they cared about. But now . . .'

'Now?' he prompted, looking up to meet her eyes.

'Now things are different,' she admitted. 'Because I met you, and Dan and Maggie and Ruth – and you all work for so little but you seem really happy there. Like it's not about having nice cars or clothes at all. You all look out for each other and for the animals. It's a happy place. And when you came with me to rescue the dog, I felt . . .'

'What?'

'I felt good. I felt I'd done something really good, for someone – something – else. It sounds stupid.'

'No, it doesn't.'

'I don't think I've ever really thought about other people or things before.' She looked up at him. 'I asked my mum to write a really big cheque for the sanctuary and I'm thinking of asking Dan if I can come to work at weekends sometimes. I'm also going to start helping Ruth's sister at her youth centre. They want me to do some design workshops. And it's all because – because of *you*, and the others. Harry – I . . . when I said I didn't think it could work between us, um . . . I was thinking of *me* and what my friends would say. But actually, I can't think why *you'd* want to go out with me because I'm – I'm vain and selfish, and you're the one who got beaten up because of me . . .' To her horror, she dissolved into tears again.

'Don't cry. Please don't cry, Lola.' Harry touched her cheek. 'I'm fine, really. And the fact that you're here – you don't know how much that means to me.'

She wiped her face. 'I look such a mess.'

'You look amazing. You always look amazing, even with black stuff on your face.' His mouth twisted. 'I thought you were gorgeous the minute I met you.'

'You did?' Her tears stopped abruptly, she was so surprised.

'Of course I did.'

'But you seemed – you hardly seemed to notice me.'

'Yeah, well, didn't want to be caught staring at you, did I? I expect you get enough of that as it is. I didn't think you'd look twice at *me*,' Harry added.

'I didn't – not to start with. But you – you're interesting.'

He smiled. 'Thanks. I'm not as pretty as your boyfriend.'

'*Ex*-boyfriend, remember?'

'Oh.' His smile grew larger, though he winced as it pulled the skin across his cheekbones. 'I forgot. That's good.'

'Yeah.' Lola felt her mouth curve in response. 'Yeah, it is good. Because now I—' Her throat clogged and she stopped.

'Now . . . ?' he prompted, his eyes fastened on hers.

Lola cleared her throat. Her voice sounded impossibly loud to her own ears. 'Now I want to go out with you.'

There was a pause.

'If – if you want to, that is . . .' Lola said, suddenly terrified. What if he'd changed his mind? 'I mean, if you don't, then . . . then it's fine, but I thought . . .'

He laughed, and then winced again. 'Ow. You idiot, of course I want to go out with you.'

'Don't call me an idiot.'

'You gorgeous, beautiful, stunning idiot,' he amended, reaching for her face. 'Is that better?'

'Suppose so . . .' said Lola, before her eyes closed and she melted into his arms.

# Chapter 18

## it's like living in a dream

'This is the best launch I've ever been to,' Sienna told her mother, gazing around at the room full of expensively-dressed people.

Lola laughed. 'You've only been to two.'

Helena smiled indulgently. 'It does look good, doesn't it? Yes.'

The hotel ballroom was huge, with six crystal chandeliers suspended from the high ceiling. Around the luxuriously decorated walls were strung garlands of ivy and pink roses, studded with twinkling fairy lights. At one end of the room a stage had been erected, on which stood an enormous fibreglass version of the 'Helena's Whisper' perfume bottle. Images of Helena herself, one finger pressed seductively to her lips, were projected onto the screen behind it. Sinuous gymnasts in pink lycra performed slow, hypnotic ballets in individual spotlights, and a woman in a silk ballgown was singing soft ballads.

Around the edges of the room were tables piled high with perfume samples, including the two already released, 'Helena's Blush' and 'Helena's Kiss'. Transparent balloons containing miniature pink heart balloons and confetti bobbed above them.

The caterers had outdone themselves too. Pink-suited waiters and waitresses brought round a selection of canapés, from smoked salmon mousse on tiny pancakes to chocolate éclairs the size of a thumb, piped full of pink cream and decorated with a swirl of white chocolate. There was also an assortment of pink sweets, from strawberry creams to jelly hearts.

'It's like living in a dream,' said Sienna, for the third time that evening.

Lola felt like that too, but not in quite the same way her sister meant it. Looking around, she was impressed by the grandeur but it no longer held quite the same spell over her. Now, she was starkly reminded of the vast contrast between the wealth of the people present and the people who worked day-in, day-out at the scruffy sanctuary. She'd also now been twice to the youth centre that

Ruth's sister Martha helped to run. At first she'd felt very uncomfortable, but the kids there were so eager to have a go at designing their own stuff that she'd soon felt like she fitted right in. There were one or two girls who showed real talent too. Lola had suggested they might all try to create some designs for a local fashion show. The idea had gone down brilliantly, and Martha told Lola she was a born teacher and artist. The compliment warmed Lola like hot chocolate – and Corin's approval of her ideas for the redesign of his club only added to the pleasure. *I really feel like my life is on track*, she thought. *Not the track I expected, but an even better one.*

Helena was in her element, drifting along in a haze of her own perfume, delicately air-kissing the models, designers, journalists, beauticians, business executives and celebrities. Murmuring, 'How wonderful of you to come!' before drifting away to talk to someone more important.

'Bet Naiha's gutted she's missing this,' Sienna commented.

Lola pulled a face. 'I don't care if she is. We're not friends any more.'

'I know, I know. Shame – she was funny.'

'Only because she went totally over the top all

the time.' Lola thought of her friends from school. Their circle was splitting; fragmenting around her. Alisha had shown an unexpected interest in helping out at the youth centre, once Lola had explained how much fun her first session had been – she and the kids could really do some good stuff together around music, she thought. Tasha, on the other hand, was spending more time with Naiha and had started dating Samir. Lola didn't mind – something fundamental had changed inside her, and things that had been important before didn't feel as important now.

Sienna interrupted her thoughts. 'All this makes my heart thump,' she said wistfully.

Lola's heart was thumping too, but not for the same reason. Any minute now, Harry was due to arrive. At first, he had refused: 'I won't know what to say. It's not my kind of thing.'

Lola had slipped her arms around his neck and said, 'Please. I want you to be my date.'

He pulled a face. 'Then we should go in together.'

'I can't, I have to get ready with my sisters. It's all been arranged. Please – please come. Everyone would like you to. Sienna's been going on about teaching you to dance.'

He was wavering. 'I haven't got anything to wear . . .'

'Now *that* I can definitely help with.'

'I don't want you to buy me stuff.'

'I won't. Corin says he's got some suits that don't fit any more. I can adjust one for you.'

Harry sighed and gave in. 'All right. But if it's grim then I'm coming straight home.'

Lola scanned the room for him, but she knew he wasn't here yet. She could sense if he was nearby or not; his presence made her tingle. She couldn't wait to see him in the suit, all smartened up.

'This is amazing,' came a voice, and Lola turned to see Ruth and Martha. The two of them looked lovely, in customized dresses that they had found in charity shops and decorated under Lola's guidance.

Lola beamed. 'I'm so pleased you could come.'

'It's like a fairy tale,' said Ruth, and blushed. 'Sorry, that sounds really daft.'

'No, it doesn't.' Martha grinned at Lola. Ruth's sister had the same white-blonde hair, though hers was cut into a severe bob, and she had six studs in each ear. 'It's all gorgeous. I'm a bit disappointed there's no red carpet, though.'

Lola burst out laughing. 'Sorry. You can't please everyone.'

'You look stunning,' said Ruth, her gaze sweeping over Lola in appreciation.

'Thanks.' Lola looked down at herself. It wasn't a new dress: after all the initial fuss about Sienna going shopping with their mother, Lola had decided she didn't need a new one after all – she had several that would do the job perfectly. It was a pale gold colour, with a lace overlay and a fishtail flick to the skirt. The bodice was decorated with tiny seed beads and the lace sleeves reached to her wrists in scalloped points. She had decided not to wear any jewellery apart from a pair of tiny gold stud earrings – the dress was embellished enough. Her hair fell loosely to her shoulders and was almost exactly the same colour as the dress.

*What will Harry think?* she couldn't help wondering. He'd never seen her dressed up like this before . . . Her eyes travelled to the grand doorway again and her heart almost stopped.

*There he is.*

She would have known him anywhere, even though he looked very different from his usual self. The suit fitted perfectly, and he'd even managed to tame his hair. He stood awkwardly in the doorway, one hand in his pocket, eyes searching the stylish crowd. Then he saw her.

Lola had always wondered if the cliché *their eyes met across a crowded room* could actually be true. Now she knew that it was. And she had never imagined it could feel like this. Everyone else faded into insignificance. The music faded into silence, until all she could hear was the sound of her own breathing, and all she could see was Harry.

He didn't look surprised at her appearance. His jaw didn't drop; he didn't gasp at her beauty. But his eyes grew warmer, and a smile spread across his face that just radiated happiness.

Curious, Ruth and Martha turned to see what Lola was staring at. 'Is that Harry?' asked Ruth, amazed. 'I'd never have recognized him!'

'I would,' said Lola, her eyes fixed on him. 'Excuse me.' Leaving the other two staring after her, she stepped down onto the dance floor and walked straight across to him. Magically, people parted in front of her and she held his gaze until she was standing in front of him. 'Hello.'

'Hello,' he said. 'You look nice.'

She laughed. 'Thanks. So do you.'

Sienna appeared at her elbow. 'Hi, Harry,' she said. 'Nice suit!'

He grinned at her. 'Thanks. I like your – er – your dress.'

Sienna, who was wearing a pale pink Marchesa mini-dress with lace overlay and a corsage at the waist, laughed. 'Thanks. Now, are you ready for that dance lesson?'

'Sienna, he's only just got here!'

Sienna raised her eyebrows. 'So?'

Lola slipped her arm through his. 'Not right now,' she told her sister. 'I'm going to be the first one to dance with my boyfriend.' The word made her tingle, and she could tell by the way Harry's arm squeezed hers against his side that he was pleased she'd said it too.

Quinn appeared, stunning in silver. 'Hello, Harry,' she said. 'I'm so glad you came. You can keep Lola out of trouble.'

'Hey!'

Quinn laughed. 'Are you hungry?'

Harry brightened. 'Starving.'

'You'll need to eat about fifty canapés to get anything like a decent meal, but there's plenty to go round.' Quinn leaned forward conspiratorially. 'The best place to be is over in the far corner. It's right next to the catering table and you can help yourself as much as you like.'

'Is *that* why you've been over there all evening?' asked Sienna, diverted.

'Of course!' Quinn patted her tummy. 'And if I'm going to be a university student, I'd better get used to party food.'

'You got in?' asked Harry.

Quinn nodded. 'I only heard this morning, but yes. They've given me a place on the physio foundation course I wanted.'

'Congratulations!'

'If you don't mind . . .' Lola interrupted. 'I was just taking my *boyfriend* to the dance floor.'

'Ooooh,' said Sienna, rolling her eyes, but Quinn shushed her, smiling.

'Off you go. Come with me, Sienna. You absolutely have to try the crab blinis.'

Lola led Harry onto the dance floor. 'You know I don't really dance . . .' he said uncertainly.

'Neither do I,' she told him. 'You just sway round and round in circles.'

'Oh – OK.' He put his arms around her waist. 'You do look gorgeous,' he said softly. 'But I guess you know that.'

'So do you.'

He grinned. 'You're a bad liar, Lola Cassidy.'

'I'm not lying.' *And I'm really not. He is gorgeous – on the outside, and on the inside too.* And she put her hands on either side of his face and drew it towards her, and kissed him, right in the middle of the most fashionable party in town, in front of all her family and friends – and it was *brilliant*.

You can meet some of the Sweet Hearts girls again
in the fantastic new book

# Deep
# Water

Available soon

Read on to find out who . . .

'Makes our centre look a bit shabby, doesn't it?' Millie whispered to Pearl as they stepped onto the luxurious carpet of the Kellerman Club foyer.

Pearl nodded. 'Totally. I mean, we've got all the up-to-date equipment, and all that, but this place – wow. Look at the chairs!'

'I love the drapes,' added Millie, looking up at the great swathes of blue chiffon that hung from the ceiling. 'Kind of underwatery.'

'We haven't come to swim,' Pearl told her with a smile. 'We've come to be *pampered*.'

Millie giggled. 'I know. I can't believe it. I've never even had my nails done before, have you?'

'No. Nor a facial. I hope it's nice.'

'In a place like this?' Millie waved an arm. 'Bound to be. Can you imagine what we'd be paying for a day here normally?'

'Good thing they're sponsoring the team, then,' interrupted Evie, overhearing. Her eyes sparkled. 'I'm having a hot stone massage, an aromatherapy facial, reflexology and a relaxation session.'

Pearl laughed. 'Got it all planned out?'

'You betcha.'

'This way!' called Jen, waving from the reception desk. 'Through to the changing rooms!'

The rest of the synchro team followed, casting admiring glances around as they went. 'I could *live* here,' declared Millie.

Pearl felt the same way. They had been to nice clubs and centres to train before, of course – sometimes the facilities abroad were amazing – but this place had a lovely atmosphere. There was a faint scent of lilies in the air, and the lighting was so subtle you couldn't even see where it was coming from. A woman in a white and blue uniform was leading the way down a wooden-panelled corridor to a white door at the end. The whole place felt calm and peaceful, rather than the streamlined, focused, high-performance environment she was used to.

Millie was practically euphoric about the changing rooms. 'Have you *seen* this?' she yelped, pulling out a long white bathrobe from her locker. 'These cost about thirty quid in Marks and Spencers! Omigosh, and flip-flops too! And an eye mask! I am *so* saving up for a subscription to this place.'

'You'd have to save for a long time,' Georgie advised her, tying back her frizzy red hair. 'I've seen the prices.'

'Remember we all have to put on the GB swim costumes to start with,' Jen called over. 'They want a photo in the lounge area, by the fishpond.'

'Fishpond?' Millie pretended to faint. 'This is all too much.'

Pearl laughed. 'Come on. Otherwise we'll be late for all that relaxing.'

The nine girls, attired in their white bathrobes and Team GB swimming costumes, filtered out of the changing room and into a large open area bordered with padded mattresses and comfy cushions. In the middle was a large sunken pond, in which koi carp could be seen lazily swimming. Pearl felt her heart beat excitedly. How many girls her age had the chance to come to a place like this? Synchro might be hard work, but it did have its benefits!

There was a photographer setting up a camera and several other people, including a tanned man in his fifties with a friendly face, and a tall blonde teenage girl standing next to him. Pearl smiled shyly at her as their gazes met, and the girl immediately beamed back and came over. 'Hi there,' she said. 'Have you got everything you need?'

'Yes thanks,' said Pearl, wondering who she was. She wasn't wearing a uniform like the other staff. 'This place is gorgeous. My friend Millie wants to live here.'

The blonde girl giggled. 'Thanks. My step-dad will be pleased.'

'Your step-dad?' Pearl glanced over towards the older man, who was chatting to the cameraman.

'Corin Kellerman,' replied the girl. 'I'm Lola. I shouldn't really be here, but I begged Corin to let me come. I think what you guys do is amazing!'

'Oh – thanks.' Pearl was a little surprised. 'Not many people know much about synchro. It's always nice to hear someone enjoys it.'

'Are you kidding? It's fantastic! I had a go once – me and my sister went on a one-day course thing. She was pretty good, actually, but I couldn't get the hang of being upside down so much.' Lola pulled a face. 'I had no idea how hard it was until we tried it.'

'That's what everyone says,' agreed Pearl. 'People think it's just floating around, making nice patterns.'

'Well, I think you're all brilliant,' Lola told her. 'And I'm so excited you're going to spend the day here. You must check out the new hot mud treatment; it's completely blissful. And make sure you get Amelia for the facial; she's the best.'

'What's this?' Millie came to join them. 'Are you getting tips, Pearl?'

'This is Millie,' Pearl said to Lola. 'She's the one who wants to live here.'

'I totally do!' exclaimed Millie. 'Everything here – I mean, you've got it all. It's like my idea of heaven. All these cushions to lie down on, and people to bring you drinks and new bathrobes – I *adore* the bathrobes – and even the stuff out in reception, all those beautiful drapes and things . . .' She sighed.

Lola blushed. 'You really like the drapes? They were my idea.'

'Really?' Millie stared at her. 'They're so pretty, like waves.'

'That's exactly the look I was going for.' Lola beamed. 'You see, Corin got this design firm in to do all the décor, but he hated everything they did, so he fired them. And then he let me have a go, and he liked my ideas miles better, so I basically did it all. The cushions, the drapes, the candles, the fragrance – all of it.'

'Wow.' Millie and Pearl looked at her with respect. 'That's really clever.'

Lola went even pinker, but she was saved from

replying by a call from the cameraman.

'Can I have everyone over here, sitting on this mat, please?'

'Talk to you later,' Lola said. 'And ask me if there's anything you want to know.' She beamed again. 'It's so exciting to meet real Olympic swimmers!'

Pearl's story continues in

# DEEP WATER

Can she swim to success in the Olympic Games?
And will she find time for romance too?

Find out in the next fantastic Sweet Hearts
story – coming Summer 2012

## 'Everyone falls in love.

Whether you're in love with the boy next door or somebody in your French class, it makes no difference to how you feel. Dare you speak to the object of your affection? What will they say? Maybe it's better not to risk it! But then you'll always wonder . . . what if?

*Sweet Hearts* are for those of you who love, have loved and will love. So, in a way, they're for everyone . . . everywhere . . . for ever. Happy dreams ever after!'

*Jo x*

# Have you read all the **Sweet Hearts** books?
## Discover the entire series

# STAR CROSSED

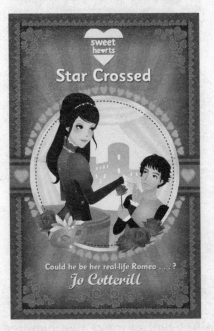

Fliss isn't exactly outgoing. But on stage
she really comes alive. And this summer,
she's playing Juliet opposite her dream
Romeo – Tom Mayerling.
If only she could tell him how she feels!

But unless Fliss finds some inner confidence,
she's going to miss her chance with Tom.
Because someone else has her eyes on Fliss's
role – and her leading man . . .

ISBN 978 1 849 41205 6

# STRICTLY FRIENDS?

Megan has had to move two hundred miles
away from her home, her dancing and her
best friend and ballroom partner, Jake.
She's fed up with having to fit in with what
everyone else wants.

Then she meets Danny. He's exciting
and rebellious and he likes her too.

But could there be more to Danny
than meets the eye?

ISBN 978 1 849 41206 3

# FORGET ME NOT

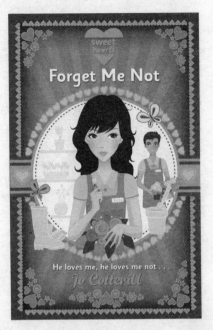

Kate Morrell used to have it all – fun, friends
and family. But since her mum died three years
ago, Kate can't remember what it's like to feel
properly happy any more.

A summer job at the local garden centre
gives Kate a chance to re-discover the spark
she once had - and arguing with her arrogant
(but gorgeous) co-worker Simon makes her
really come out of her shell!

But then there's an attack on the
centre – and Kate begins to wonder if
Simon knows more than he's letting on . . .

ISBN 978 1 849 41217 9

# ICE DREAMS

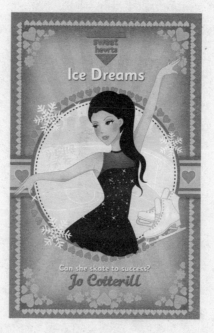

Ice skating is Tania's life – she's a champion
in the making. But things have started
to go wrong and she can't tell anyone why
she's become scared of the ice.

When her coach tells her she's got to pair up with
someone, Tania is furious. Zac is a daredevil, a
skater with no fear – and she doesn't trust him.

Rebel meets ice queen - watch out,
the sparks will fly!

ISBN 978 1 849 41216 2

# DEEP WATER

Pearl can't believe her luck when she's selected
for the British Synchronized Swimming team,
competing at the 2012 Olympics in London.
It's a dream come true!

But being an Olympian is hard work.
Non-stop training means less time for friends
and fun — a sacrifice Pearl is willing to make if
it means her team can bring home a medal . . .
She's determined that even the cheeky journalist
Bailey won't distract her from going for gold.
But he has other ideas!

ISBN 978 1 849 41219 3

## Go to